THIS SECOND EDITION IS DEDICATED TO THOSE MORE THAN FIVE-HUNDRED-THOUSAND NAMELESS ALBANIANS WHO GAVE SO MUCH AND ASKED FOR SO LITTLE IN RETURN. THEY HAVE BECOME THE MAIN PILLAR TO A NATIONAL AND CULTURAL HERITAGE TO DEMONSTRATE TO THE WORLD THAT ALBANIANS ARE THE MOST GIFTED AND TALENTED INDIVIDUALS IN A PROPER SETTING. AWAY FROM THE CURRENT ALBANIAN POLITICAL RULING CAST. WHEN HISTORY DECIDES TO OPEN ITS BOOKS WITH OBJECTIVITY, THEIR NAMES – ALL FIVE-HUNDRED THOUSAND OF THEM – WILL BE IMMORTALLY ENGRAVED IN THE MINDS OF THOSE WHO MATTER. THEY ARE AN ASSET TO WHICHEVER CIVILIZATION THEY HAVE IMMIGRATED TO.

THIS DEDICATION IS NOT AND SHOULD NOT BE INTERPRETED AS POLITICAL. IT IS A LITERARY WORK'S JOB TO CONVEY A MESSAGE TO THE WORLD'S CONSCIENCE THAT GOVERNMENTAL ABUSE CAN AND MAY DESTROY THE FUTURE OF A NATION.

KLAJD GAZULLI

The Last Whisper

The Second Edition

By Klajd Gazulli

Foreword by

Michael Jackson

Designed by Main Street Publishing House

Written by Klajd Gazulli

Edited by Michael Jackson

Copyrighted © with Library of Congress and protected by United States Copyright Laws. US Copyright Office 101 Independence Ave SE Washington, DC 20559-6000

Paperback ISBN: 978-0-578-32063-2

1. American Literature 2. Romance 3. Politics 4. Art 5. Opera 6. Philosophy

Foreword

The Last Whisper is a sweeping novel, stretching across thousands of miles and dozens of years that explores love's power, persistence and sometimes its pain. How does true love endure across time and space in the face of oppression and cruelty? When does the life-sustaining power of one's nostalgic memories begin to poison any chance of an enjoyable present and hopeful future? These are the kinds of questions, "*The Last Whisper*" challenges the reader to grapple with, from its opening paragraph to its poignant ending.

This compelling journey of love, life, and loss greatly comforted me after the sudden illness and death of my late wife Anjela to cancer. Gripped by sorrow and cynicism, *The Last Whisper* reminded me that as much as love can hurt, it is ultimately what gives life meaning. Francis' journey taught me that time, distance, and even death itself are no match for the abiding power of love.

Michael Jackson

Editor of Black Intellect Journal

Who is Francis Petrela?

To understand The Last Whisper, one must make a conscientious effort to understand its main protagonist. Who is Francis Petrela?

Francis Petrela is a thinker, an intellectual and an artist who would not have it any other way. He would want us all to understand him. The points that he's trying to make.

As an Albanian-American, born in Brooklyn in 1922, born of two Albanian emigres, he fell in love with Albania, the homeland of his parents, when visiting it for the first time in 1941. He visited sites such as the Monastery of the Forty Saints, the Island of Ksamil, the Blue Eye, the ancient city of Butrint.

This heart-wrenching tale set in two different countries and during three different timeframes captures the power of never-ending love, unconditional and as pure as the souls of the two protagonists to this epic love story.

The scenes are extraordinarily depictive, capturing the beauty of Lake George, the southern coasts of Albania, and the city that never sleeps, New York. Without a doubt, Albania would capture his heart in 1941 and soon thereafter, Francis made it his home for the next thirty years.

Nonetheless, with the passing of the years, he would eventually realize that a dreamer and an intellectual could never survive the harsh realities set against a political background dominated by a one-party system in post-WWII Albania. His story will speak for itself. With subtleties and explicit images, both at the same time.

Now away from the story. Unfortunately, Albania finds itself in a somewhat comparable situation at the turn of the third decade of the 21st century. With the diminishing role of the Albanian political opposition since 2013, the Party in power has turned Albania's institutions into a grotesquely ambiguous venue to promote a one-party agenda. In the process, unilateral decisions have been made, Albania has been dubbed as the Colombia in the heart of Europe, almost all national and local government institutions have been controlled by those few at the very top, electoral processes have been manipulated, and much more. But most importantly, the harshness of such political situation combined with government's refusal to acknowledge real-life, difficult day-to-day problems has forced more than 500,000 Albanians to leave their country for a better life in the West. A nation is on the brink of losing its identity.

Ayn Rand once depicted the dangers of losing the brain and the intellectual capacities of a nation through her masterpiece "Atlas Shrugged." Her philosophical approach to "Who is John Galt" briefly meant that a government mandating and dictating the will and power of its individual citizens risks losing its human assets indefinitely. Such is the dire reality in Albania today: government subjectivity overpowering individual freedoms and choices.

The parallels between the philosophy of John Galt and that of Francis Petrela with respect to individual achievements, openness to societal incentives, minimal government interference, individual rights and civil liberties are strikingly clear.

In short, Francis' story is not his – alone. In a John Galtian way, his story belongs to the more than 500,000 Albanians, extraordinary citizens, and intellectual assets – a drain to Albania (of historic proportions) but a gain for the Western civilizations where they live and contribute tirelessly. His story should serve as a reminder that terrible situations can and may always repeat themselves. In the words of Ronald Reagan, "Freedom is never more than one generation away from extinction."

December 2020

The Author

Words from the Author

There are stories that are borne completely from ancient legends. This is not one of them. However, you may find this story bears some slight resemblance to the legendary tale of a dying man, who refused to let his life fade away without whispering a few poignant words to his family. Words of unconditional love and sacrifice.

It is late at night. A steamy hot summer night in 2003. I am sitting down in a small café, overlooking the beautiful orange tones of the Sun as they gently caress the Ionian coastal waters of southern Albania. Vivid images of an old lady, with whom I had spoken briefly during my stay, appear before my eyes. She looks lost and impoverished, and I feel bad for her. She is almost 80.

I met her when I first arrived early in the summer. Though I hadn't visited Albania in almost 10 years, my instincts told me that this summer was going to be quite unique. I packed some of my belongings and took the first flight out of New York's JFK airport. Upon arriving at the Albania capital city of Tirana, I mentioned to my relatives that I would be traveling to the scenic southern coastal town of Saranda. The first thing many of them said was "Go see the Blue Eye." So, I went to see the popular tourist attraction nestled near the tiny village of Muzine. The view of the crystal-clear blue waters of this ancient spring gently flowing into the Bistrice River was breathtaking. Picturesque. I immediately took out a small notepad from my bag and began to jot down some of my thoughts and observations.

"Beautiful, isn't it?" said a voice from behind me.

I turned back and saw the old lady. It was our first-time meeting.

"Pardon me, ma'am?" I replied.

"It is beautiful. Don't you think so?"

The first thing that came to mind was that she was obviously not native to the area, given her American English accent.

"Without a doubt," I answered.

"Do you write?" asked the old lady, looking at the notepad.

"I can barely put two words together. But I do write small notes here and there."

"Small notes?" asked the old lady, with tears almost instantly coming to her eyes. "I am sorry. It reminds me of someone," she added.

We spoke a little longer and to be honest she tugged at my heartstrings. Her name was Celeste. I found out that she lives along Lake George, a popular resort area in upstate New York, and was only in Albania for two or so more weeks. Since she was going to go back so soon, she invited me to visit her upon my return to New York. She said she wanted to tell me a story. A story she'd never told anyone before.

Stories of the heart have always intrigued me, so of course, I enthusiastically accepted her offer. A month after returning to the States from Albania, I drove the four hours to her house along Lake George. She looked just as gracious as she had the first time we met at the Blue Eye. She showed me her journals, notes, letters. She told me anecdotes, stories, heartbreaking decisions she had made. She cried as she did so. It was right around the Fourth of July holiday. A date incredibly special to her and to the memory of her loved ones.

By the time Celeste finished telling me her story, she said: "I know you told me that you can't put two words together. But please, try to write about this. I would hate for this story to die with me. Francis was all I ever had and all I ever wanted."

Thick tears formed beneath her wrinkled eyelids. As I listened to her voice, heartbreakingly heavy with the memories of her many years, I became deeply attached to her story.

Here I am now, less than a month after hearing about her past, back along the southern coasts of Albania. I hadn't planned to visit this quickly, but the devotion Celeste had to her past made it impossible for me to stay away. This café, a mere thirty-seven-minute drive away from the Blue Eye, provides the first stop on my journey to reconstruct the loving story of two people completely devoted to each other. Francis, or St. Francis as she always endearingly referred to him, had been the love of her life. He was a cellist when they met in 1939. She was a ballerina.

I abruptly grab my glass and down the last drop of bourbon. "Here's to two wonderful people," I think to myself as I offer the two lovers a solitary toast of admiration.

Their story is a recollection of anecdotes, letters, short notes, journals, and sheer observations. Here and there, I may fill in the blanks with my own voice. But without a doubt, this is their story of love and not a tale of pity or pain. For love itself is as eternal as the memory of these two wonderful human beings. In a way, their story is interconnected to another: the legendary tale of a dying man who saved his last breath to whisper a few remaining words.

I stare intently at my now empty glass. No more bourbon. I put on my New York Yankees baseball hat and stare at the beautifully unreachable horizon as it appears to extend millions of miles away. I walk and wonder if I could ever love someone as deeply as these two loved each other. Gut-wrenchingly painful. Impossibly never-ending.

I walk on. I walk on, distraught by their pain, fueled by their love…

Thus, I embark on my journey to tell this story. A journey I will walk for the next 10 years. The story of the last whisper.

July 4, 2013

Prologue

The contents of the last chapter of Francis' journal came as a surprise to her. It was not that she didn't know that people were capable of living for as long as he did; but with the sheer number of adventurous years consumed during Francis' life, she thought it would be particularly impossible. Given life's relatively short timeframe, coupled with his own physical limitations, one could not blame her for thinking the final events of his last chapter improbable.

She was not shocked by its author's persistence though. In a way, it was befitting and reminiscent of a story she heard long ago. As a young girl, she was told of a legendary tale, the tale of an old dying man who saved his last breath to whisper a few last words of love to his family. Though fully aware of his unavoidably impending demise, this man, a warrior of sorts, refused to fade away into the great unknown until he could speak to his loved ones about all the things that had weighed heavily upon his heart.

Celeste had first read Francis' last chapter years ago on this date, the Fourth of July. To her, such a chapter was more than simply a beautifully written ending to a life filled with copious amounts of love and hardships. It was a testament. It was proof that legendary tales are not merely foolish myths, but rather stories based on folk culture and lived experiences. The truth is that, in life as in literature, every chapter epitomizes the totality of its author; in every word, one could almost hear his last whisper.

Today, four years to the day, after initially learning of the old man's heartfelt whispered words, Celeste still finds herself reading his last chapter. She decided to read it precisely on this day to remind herself that scientific rationality can only go so far and then miracles happen. "What science cannot explain, love justifies," she thinks time and time again.

Her name is Celeste Salek, an elderly seventy-nine-year-old woman. However, for more than sixty years, she has awaited this day with the breathless anticipation of a teenage girl. Each year, she looks forward to this one day. She does so not for the annual holiday's remembrance of young men and women who sacrificed their lives to give birth to this great nation during the American Revolutionary War. She does so instead because she has a promise to fulfill. She is on a personal crusade. No matter how long it may take or how overwhelming it may be, Celeste is determined to see it through to the end. It has to do with 'the final chapter;' its concept always evokes feelings of mystery and obligation in her. There is one thing that is not a mystery though: each year, with a week to go until the momentous date, she starts counting down the days. Each time this publicly commemorative, yet personally elusive day comes to an end, she feels the same deep pain. It's as if a part of her leaves with the passing of each Fourth of July; her promise again is beyond her reach, mercilessly disappearing into the cracks of time.

Why of all the days, does she choose this one to be a monumental symbol of her past? Why select this one day to act as the proper time for fulfilling a promise? Does the reason rest solely on 'the final chapter'? Or does she have an alternative justification for this tradition?

"The Gods of Independence will not have it any other way," Celeste playfully convinces herself each year as she begins her annual rituals.

It is the Fourth of July holiday in America. A day which marks the birth of a nation and a reminder of the revolutionary sacrifices of its sons and daughters. Millions around the country observe it by joyously gathering with family and friends, while happily enjoying food and drinks. This jubilant holiday commemorates not only lost lives and selfless deeds, but it also proclaims that, throughout the nation's history, its vigilance and dedication to liberty has not died.

A still-grieving mother across the street remembers how her only son was killed during the war in Vietnam, despite the months that have passed since Memorial Day. Two doors down, an elderly man fondly recalls his role in the heroic battle in Normandy. There, he risked his life to liberate the world from the tyrannical Nazi war machine's suffocating grip on all of humankind. The owner of the retail store, down the block, delightfully labors to fully stock his store's inventory with essential everyday items that will satisfy his loyal customers. Children in the neighborhood park scream with joy, knowing that the town's huge annual fireworks display is only hours away. However, among these traditional holiday activities, someone – somewhere – embraces this day for other more personal reasons.

For Celeste, this is no different; apart from fulfilling her promise, this day presents a unique gift – something meticulously wrapped in the layers of the past. Each year she never forgets to comb through these layers and try to unfold them. Because she knows that doing so always provides her with a long since forgotten feeling. And every year that this day comes to its inevitable, yet surprisingly abrupt conclusion, Celeste fully soaks in the innumerable memories of years gone by. Each wrinkle in her beautiful, yet time-worn face tells its own story.

Celeste picks up her hardcover journal from the nightstand. She reverently holds it in her hands as if it is a religious tome imbued with magical powers. In it, she finds consolation, a reason to believe that miracles can happen, that they are often ingrained in the most unimaginable places. What sort of miracles? Though of that she remains unsure, she has long since accepted the veracity of this belief.

While holding the journal in her hands, Celeste turns to look at the statue of Saint Francis sitting on the shelf, tears immediately begin pouring from her eyes. She can't seem to make them stop and feels so miserably lost in this vulnerable emotional state. The only possible escape from this emotional entrapment would be for her to refuse to submit to this yearly ritual.

Despite all this pain and heartache, Celeste cannot and will not stop fighting through her feelings, for unconditional love never surrenders. She knows that reading excerpts from the ailing man's final chapter will, yet again, emotionally torment her throughout the day and well into the night. Yet, she feels a strong sense of duty and obligation, and not of a ritualized habit. Once again, Celeste commits to reading this final chapter, for the words always whisper the sound of truth.

With her watery eyes glued to the scene of the intoxicatingly serene surface of Lake George, Celeste holds the journal which contains important matters and secrets of the heart. At that moment, she spontaneously opens the journal to a page bookmarked with a single folded piece of paper. She unfolds it and begins to read…

You understand the universal truth that our individual lives are not profound stories attempting to change the world. Nor are they sorrowful tales of defeat or pity. A life does not make excuses with hypothetical 'could haves,' 'should haves,' and 'would haves.' This is a 'boy meets girl' story of sacrifice and unconditional love. It is also ultimately a simple, elusive, intangible mirage of a past long gone…

Celeste stops reading, looks up, and stares through her reading glasses out of her large window. She stands up, walks towards the large old window which overlooks Lake George, and slowly sits in her favorite chair next to the window. She stares beyond the leafy bushes, huge trees, and all the spacious areas in between while remembering all the intimate details. Details that have been passed down to her through the years by others recounting their own memories, contemporaneously written journals, and from her own personal experiences.

All these things evoke the same sentiments as the words written in the folded letter, which she has just moments ago ceased reading; sentiments uniquely heart wrenching and eternally impactful; memorable and alluring; joyous and sorrowful.

Celeste opens the journal to another page. There she finds a grainy black and white picture and touches it gently. In her hands, she holds an old photograph that has become tattered at the corners and partially stained throughout the years. She affectionately caresses the contours of the man's mysterious face on the photo. A face as mysterious as her own past. The photo depicts a handsome young man assuming a pose so indecipherable it could be variously interpreted, depending on the picture's context, and the observer's perspective. The pose conveys equal parts intimacy and indifference, as much a sense of closeness as aloofness. At least, that is how Celeste sees it; that is how she's always seen it. While considering all these seemingly contradictory feelings, she wonders, how one man can personify all these opposing qualities in a single photograph.

One of the great paradoxes of Celeste's long life has been her struggle to understand the collision between diametrically opposing truths. Long ago, she accepted the reality that in life two contradictory feelings can find ways to coexist, though never intellectually grasping the exact mechanics behind this peculiar harmony. She's simply embraced the reality that such a harmony exists, without investigating the individual aspects of life that support that existence. In many ways, this approach helped her at various points in her life, for it enabled her to overcome life's often unbearable obstacles without getting stuck in the overwhelming minutia of the moment.

In the moments before Celeste is about to thumb through the rest of the journal and read its final chapter, an extensive monologue by none other than the mysterious man in the photograph, she pauses. Instead, she decides to rest the journal on her lap, then looks again through the window to the idyllic images beyond.

Like the image in the old photograph, showing a man who appears to be thinking simultaneously of the past, present, and future, Celeste sits with the thick locks of her nearly white hair pressed against the window frame. Her position next to the window somehow helps peel away the many events of a long lifetime of memories.

A stunningly vintage beauty in her own right, Celeste remains thoughtfully still, almost as if frozen in the river of time. Her thoughts drift away on this Fourth of July, as they do every Fourth of July, wishing that perhaps this year, this Independence Day will bring with it a long-desired sense of fulfillment, of restful finality. Miracles can happen, she keeps thinking to herself. She hopes that on this day, the past will finally reclaim her and embrace her in its arms…

Francis Petrela

It was September 1969, and a group of young children was seated in a small classroom while a cool early Autumn breeze crept in through the shattered windows. Red scarves were wrapped around their shallow shoulders and knotted near their necklines in honor of their revered Communist leader. With their tiny hands, they shuffled through their papers and textbooks, trying to ready themselves for the final period of the day. Now they intently watched their teacher as he slowly wrote the words "Music Hour" in chalk on the blackboard. It was stained, much as the walls of the classroom, with moisture accumulated over its many years of use.

Despite its unkempt appearance and unsanitary conditions, the classroom still resembled a small art gallery and had become the only world the children knew and appreciated. It was a place where they took the first steps on their journey toward knowledge and understanding, where their young minds had been molded by newly learned ideas and concepts. It was understood that, within the confines of these walls and under the teacher's calculated supervision, kids could remain uncorrupted and feel somewhat liberated; they showed that they were unafraid to express themselves by displaying boundless imagination.

There were almost imperceptible whispers radiating from the back of the classroom. The teacher, Francis Petrela, quickly quelled the ambient whispers: "Quiet please!" His rich tenor voice bellowed out like that of Italian singer Enrico Caruso. And though the teacher's voice might have been slightly deeper than the operatic virtuoso, both men shared similarly dignified ways of speaking, both in eloquence and mannerism.

Francis turned to his students and intensely gazed at them one by one; his brown eyes gleaming with the sunlight that poured through the room's windows. He placed the instructor's guide on his desk and picked up a piece of paper with a list which was divided into several sections. Those pupils who were present in the class were marked as such in the attendance section. One student was missing.

The students had kept their usual seats over the last four years. Over that time, their teacher had taught many other subjects in addition to music. He taught them about rich Albanian language and history, math, and geography among other subjects. Francis had inspired them to learn with his patient approach. He loved watching them grow into fine young people; each one of them held a special place in his heart.

Yet, there was one child that he had inspired the most. His name was Agron, the same student that was currently absent from class. During his first year in school, Agron had repeatedly forgotten homework assignments and yet Francis still exercised an overwhelming patience with him. One day, a couple of years ago, the teacher had given the class an assignment to write a short story describing their first day back to school. Agron's story was strewn with poor grammar and sloppy sentence structure. Despite this, the teacher could recognize that his ideas were unprecedently original for a child his age. So instead of sternly criticizing the substandard structure and grammar, the teacher congratulated him for his effort. Agron's eyes gleamed with happiness and pride when the teacher remarked: "Your ideas are unique and brilliant!" That precise moment became a turning point for Agron.

But today, Agron's absence made him feel concerned. Francis was quite worried. Until today, the young student had never missed a class and had always been a consistently active participant in class discussions. The teacher looked at Agron's name one more time in hopes that the young boy would soon walk through the door.

Francis looked up from the attendance sheet and at the empty seat; this space that had not been without a child's eager presence for as long as he'd been teaching at this school. Where is he? Why has he missed the whole day of school? Has anyone seen him?

As the increasingly worried instructor was about to ask the class if they had seen him, someone knocked on the door.

"Come in," the teacher commanded with a soothing voice.

The door slowly opened and in walked a young boy with his head lowered. He was wearing a long-sleeved cotton shirt and velvet pants torn a bit near the ankles.

"I apologize for my lateness."

Agron's face looked torrid. His eyes, still wet with tears, looked puffy and bloodshot. His hair was unkempt, and his very presence exuded a feeling of helplessness. He was not wearing the red scarf that had become a synonymous symbol for all his peers.

"It is alright Agron. Take your seat and open your textbook to page seventeen."

Francis looked at the boy, slowly walking to his desk in the back of the classroom, with a strong sense of sympathy. Agron's uncharacteristic tardiness and disheveled appearance must have something to do with his missing red scarf, the teacher thought.

After the boy finally took a seat, Francis marked him present for class on the attendance sheet and looked up from the podium again, but this time with intentions of finally starting the class discussion for the day.

"Alright! Can anyone remind us again why music is important?"

The usual eager students raised their hands and waited their turn to respond. "We sing to our glorious Party," said one pupil. "We hail to our national heroes," answered another. They all gave reasons straight out of the textbook as Francis silently and half-heartedly accepted their unimaginative considerations of music.

"They are all good answers," he said, not at all certain how convincing his reply had sounded. "What about you Agron? Can you give us another reason?"

The young boy, with tear-filled eyes, looked around at all his peers. In a voice rife with nervousness and probably a bit of intimidation, he stumblingly murmured a few incomprehensible words.

"Louder please," the teacher asserted.

Suddenly the young student, summoning within him adequate mental and emotional fortitude, spoke with a steady audible pitch.

"Yes, we sing to our Party and our national heroes. We sing to our history and culture. But we also sing about good things and bad things, about things which are beautiful and things which are ugly. We sing about our joys and sorrows, about love and hatred. We sing about all our feelings and experiences. Because you see…" Agron paused for a moment, stared at his beloved teacher, from whom he had gained inspiration, and said, "Music is the rhythm of life."

The entire class became eerily silent for a moment, with most student's eyes bulging in disbelief. Then, suddenly, they broke out in a unified show of approval that steadily increased both in pitch and tempo with each acclamation: "Rhythm of life! Rhythm of life!"

The teacher looked at Agron with amazement and a pride-filled smile on his face. His heart filled with joy, seeing how fine a student his pupil had become. Agron had grown into a boy with the sharp mind of a writer or even a poet. When the class's cheers subdued and matched the teacher's prolonged silence, Francis, with a piece of white chalk in his hand, stood up from his desk and began to slowly write the words on the blackboard: "Rhythm of life!"

The teacher also wrote a huge exclamation mark on the chalkboard after those three exuberantly chanted words. Francis paused for a moment and said: "Very well! You all have half an hour to write about how music has individually impacted each of you. Don't write more than one page because I'm not planning on spending my whole night reading your life stories."

The students all burst out into joyful laughter and immediately began to busily write their new assignment. Francis roamed around the now silent classroom, observing the children with intensely curious eyes.

Every one of them remained acutely absorbed in their writing until the final bell rang.

As the class bell signaled the end of school, the students began to exit the classroom one at a time. When Agron was finally the only student left, he slowly approached the teacher and said, "I apologize again for being late."

"It's alright. What happened though? Why were you upset?" the teacher asked with his typical soft and resonant voice, while nonchalantly putting his instructor's textbook, attendance sheet, and various pens in his briefcase.

"The principal hit me for not wearing my scarf," the young boy answered with a bird-like chirping voice. His innocent eyes were filled with a shameful humility which was reminiscent of a fragile sparrow. Agron looked away, anticipating his teacher's scolding remarks. "I hope you don't think less of me, now that you know that my scarf was the reason I was disciplined."

The caring teacher neither advised him nor admonished him. Instead, Francis patted the nervous boy's head and tiny shoulders and looked him in the eyes with affection and admiration.

"Go home and try not to think about today. You will feel better tomorrow," said the teacher.

"But I didn't do it on purpose!" exclaimed the boy, this time with a more apologetically determined voice.

"I know you did not do it on purpose son!" Francis was perplexed by the child's choice of words, struggling to grasp both the totality of the situation and the boy's reason for making such an exclamation.

"I am sorry for the trouble," replied Agron, lowering his eyes with palpable humility.

"Son, there is no need to be sorry. You have not caused any trouble at all. It is just that…" the teacher remained motionless. "There are some matters that should best be left unmentioned, but you will understand this only with time."

Agron stood there with bolts of tears hanging from his eyelids, wishing that for once, some adult would recognize his maturity despite his age. The teacher's heart ached with sorrow, knowing that Agron had been demoralized and disappointed by the cruel actions and empty rhetoric of someone who was supposed to be a role model. The principal should be a protector of young children unable to stand up for themselves, not a tormentor.

But Francis knew his grim advice to Agron had unfortunately been completely true. Some things in life, for the betterment of the collective group, should remain unsaid until an appropriate time and place. Right now, was neither the time nor the place for them to remedy an injustice with righteous indignation.

"Would you tell your father to come to my house later when he has time?" Francis said as Agron was about to leave the classroom.

Upon hearing his words, Agron stopped, faced his teacher and nodded in approval. It appeared that his fear and anxiety had lividly colored his cheeks. Then the sad boy exited the classroom precisely as he had entered an hour before. His slouched thin frame disappearing from the doorway as if the weight of an unjust world had been placed on his young shoulders.

Francis was saddened to witness Agron depart with such visible discomfort. He was convinced that Agron had been emotionally scarred, because of the possible repercussions that Francis assumed would soon follow. There is a basic reality about children; one tiny, almost imperceptible, display of emotion can reveal a great deal about their true feelings. For Agron, it had exposed his innocence and naïveté, his lack of a devious or manipulative nature, and that he was extremely upset. Young children are a fountain of emotions waiting to pour out. Unlike most adults, children are more visibly demonstrative of their dissatisfaction and are generally not in the least subtle in their displays of the full gamut of human emotions.

Francis strongly felt he had failed his young student, banishing him from the safety and security of the classroom, and desecrating his sacred trust. The teacher felt that he had trampled on the delicate trust Agron had bestowed upon him. The highest honor an inspiring role model can be granted by a child is gratitude. Along with this honor, the child assigns this person the role of guardian and protector. Francis felt deeply sorry that he had not adequately upheld neither that honor nor that role. He knew that his empty rhetoric was a cop out and wished he'd shown more emotional intimacy, more consideration of Agron's distress. Now his palpable regret had unleashed in him a strong sense of determination to take these matters into his own hands. Francis was now committed to enshrining some much-needed light into the cloudy world of Agron's uncorrupted mind. He decided it was time to act and confront the principal.

As Francis came to this sudden and profound realization, he looked around the room once again. He carefully put the small stack of notebook papers, on which the students had written their responses to the class assignment, into his worn leather briefcase. Finally, he slowly walked out of the classroom and left behind another day of teaching.

A Stop at the Local Tavern

It was still early afternoon. Francis headed to the small local tavern, located not far from one of his favorite places to relax, the Blue Eye.

Moments ago, he left a heated exchange with the school principal, who incredibly argued that children are the property of the State and thus neglecting to wear the red scarf, a symbol of the State, was quite a serious matter. "Serious matter, for who?" Francis angrily asked. "Franc Petrela! These kinds of questions are in direct violation of the Party's teachings. This is intolerable!"

Francis furiously stormed out of the office feeling completely appalled with the principal's illogical treatment for a dress code violation.

The argument made him stop by the local tavern to cool off before going home. Francis wasn't that crazy about the place. However, he liked the bartender, a nice guy with whom he'd often pleasantly engage in small talk. So daily, Francis had made a routine of stopping by the tavern after the school day's last bell.

As soon as Francis walked in, he took a good long look around. The tavern was quite empty with only three or four people seated inside. The entire area was filled with a haze of cigarette smoke. Apparently, one of the patrons had decided to smoke like a chimney. Francis walked straight to the nearest barstool and sat down.

"Double cognac," he told the bartender while holding up two fingers. "Throw a couple of ice cubes in there too."

The bartender immediately began making a small glass of cognac while Francis sat patiently at the bar.

"There you go," the bartender slid the drink across the bar. "No ice cubes though," he remarked.

Francis gulped down the drink at once as if washing away the day's aggravation.

"Another one please!"

The bartender stared at him, at first, in confusion. Then, said nothing and looked at Francis with scolding eyes, clearly conveying that Francis should stop drinking.

"What's the matter, Andrea? Is the bar closed or something? Hit me up with another double cognac. Grab one for yourself too."

"I'm trying to cut down on alcohol," the bartender responded while pouring another double cognac in the teacher's glass.

"Nothing bad has ever come from alcohol," Francis said in a resolute voice. "Problems will get to you before alcohol does."

"Are you alright?" Andrea asked with concern while pouring a drink for himself in another glass.

"Of course. Couldn't be better than this," Francis answered, holding up the glass for a toast.

"Cheers!" the still concerned bartender said, as he too held his glass in salute.

"To the poor!" the teacher toasted in return. "Or better yet, here's to all the incompetent people in the world who ruin progress!"

"Shush... not so loud," the bartender looked around cunningly. "You'll get us in trouble."

Francis turned his head and again, looked around the tavern over his shoulder. This is the place where every sinner, gambler, degenerate, artisan, vagrant, and dreamer end up for one reason or another. This is where the vast multitudes of the poor come in hopes of washing away their troubles.

"Where's your friend?" the bartender asked. "I haven't seen him in a while."

"Who?" Francis asked.

"You know who. Why ask as if you don't know?" Andrea joked. "You're always around with the same person."

"Oh… you mean Nikolla. He's around. Just that he's got a lot of fish to catch. He's a true fisherman… you know."

"I didn't know that he catches fish," the bartender responded with a perplexed tone. "I thought he only unloads stuff at the docks."

"The things that he unloads are fish. He has to catch them before he unloads them though."

The bartender abruptly laughed out loud.

"I don't know about you sometimes. At times, you are serious. At times, you are not."

"I agree with you on that. Sometimes, I don't know about me either," Francis jokingly replied while placing his money on the bar. "I have to go, Andrea. A lot of work to do."

"Take it easy!"

The bartender smiled inside, watching the teacher leave. His conversations with Francis were always brief, but always funny.

The Dreamer

It was early evening as Francis watched from a distance as gentle waves caressed the rocky shoreline of the Albanian countryside. He marveled at the huge rocks along the beach and how the sunlight beautifully reflected the movement of the calming sea onto them. The Sun slowly sank below the western corner of the horizon, precisely where the velvety azure sky touched the farthest reaches of the Ionian Sea. The warm sunset colors reflected upon the darkening shadows of the blue water, creating a heavenly kaleidoscope. The panoramic view of the sea, the colorful variety of the local flora, and the gentle weather were among the many things that made the sleepy town of Saranda simply remarkable and characteristically Mediterranean.

Francis always enjoyed sitting here at night, especially after a long day of teaching. He always wondered whether natives of Saranda ever considered this town a secret paradise the same way its visitors do. He was so glad that, of all the places across Albania, he'd chosen this picturesque town to be his home.

Except for a six-year period when he briefly chased fame in Tirana, Francis had been living on the beautiful southern shores of Saranda since 1941. He had settled quite comfortably into this 150-year-old one-storied home.

Like most of the houses in southern Albania, the building's exterior was built with carved stones and its rooftop with stone shingles. When Francis discovered it, the ravages of time and its neglectful previous owners had cruelly worn down much of the old house. However, Francis managed to renovate it a bit by replacing the collapsed shingles on the roof and rebuilding the three sides of the stone walls lining the small parcel of land on which the house sat. Despite all this hard work, Francis knew he couldn't have found a better place to call home.

The layout of the town was impeccably designed. It was a perfect blending of new buildings, old taverns, tiny cafes and shops, and homes built in the age-old traditional stone style.

Legend had it that the town was named after the 'Forty Saints,' a group of martyred Christian monks who were decapitated by the conquering Turks for refusing to convert to Islam. This short, centuries-old tale had a powerful meaning for the locals. After the Communist Party took over the government in Albania, the worship of any religion had slowly become a forbidden fruit with potentially fatal implications.

Despite this demoralizingly oppressive regime, the people of Saranda walked with their heads held high, profoundly proud of the strength of their historic name. The town was even prouder of the affectionate, cheerful, and hospitable character of its people.

Francis spent most of his evenings drinking and talking politics with his friend Nikolla. Nikolla was a fifty-two-year-old, soft-spokenly articulate man from Kosovo. He had emigrated to southern Albania in 1945, right after World War II.

Usually, Nikolla would initiate their political conversations. Francis was not interested in discussing different political ideologies, but more intrigued by talking about human condition, people's connections to each other, and how individuals expressed their humanity through life-altering decisions. Francis had fought valiantly for the Albanian National Front during the war. He believed he was fighting for liberty and individual freedom against the Fascists and Nazis. But when the war ended, political butchery and oppression by the Communist Party triumphed over the humanity of his fellow Albanians.

The Albanian Communist Party, with the intentions of establishing a totalitarian state, made sure that all domestic political opposition was destroyed. Legal trials to purge political dissension, summary executions, and censorship of the arts were all tools they effectively used to achieve total control. For nearly all its citizens, the world beyond the Albanian borders became a strange and unreachable fantasy. The Communists, upon taking complete power in the country, enforced its so-called 'iron curtain' by closing Albania's borders, controlling what information could cross the border, and jailing those suspected of having 'western influences.' This drastically isolated and virtually imprisoned this small, beautiful nation and its people from the outside world.

Francis became extremely disillusioned with the recent chain of political events that he felt were suffocating the true spirit of the Albanian people. He believed Albania would only have a tremendous opportunity to flourish through political pluralism, free and active economic cooperation with the West, tolerance for a wide spectrum of musical and artistic tastes, and access to uncensored and free-thinking literature.

However, Nikolla had a different take on things. He always spoke of how proud he was to have come to Albania. "I would rather struggle in the iron fist of the Albanian leadership than flourish in the flowery and pretentious arms of a foreign oppressor," he would always say.

Although Francis would never agree with his friend's glowing assessment of communist Albania, he would pause to consider the broader picture. He understood Nikolla's feelings of dismay for Yugoslavia and its merciless grip on the ethnic Albanian lands of Kosovo.

Nikolla's entire family, including his two younger sisters, had been murdered by the Yugoslav Army during a premeditated retreat by several of their divisions. The so-called 'retreat' had been orchestrated to justify the army's planned ethnic cleansing of Kosovar Albanians. Like they did with thousands of others, several unnamed people falsely accused Nikolla's father of having collaborated with the Nazis during the war and used these accusations to murder Nikolla's whole family.

Completely devastated by such a huge loss, Nikolla traveled through the ruins of Kosovo for days, trying to escape from being another atrocity victim. After finally crossing the Albanian border, Nikolla knelt and kissed the same soil that many Renaissance poets had praised for years. "For you Albania, Kosovo sacrificed all her sons."

The brutally premeditated ethnic assassinations obliged Nikolla to search for a new family. A family that didn't seek to replace his lost loved ones, yet one that filled the void left in his heart. In 1949 he began to build a new home. He met and later married a beautiful woman who was native to Saranda. Ten years later, the couple had a baby boy and named him Agron.

Francis admired how Nikolla had persevered and triumphed over all these negative obstacles in his life. "When all seemed lost and gone," he thought, "Nikolla heard the trumpets of hope play once more. He had grabbed and held tight to his only remaining lifeline, his dream of a life in southern Albania."

On early mornings, the two of them would go fishing by the jagged rocks along the shore. Francis would tell Nikolla about his old life on the other side of the Atlantic. He would recall memories of New York City, describing in vivid detail the big city where he was born and raised. Its sights and sounds were still very fresh in Francis' mind; the streets filled with large fin-tailed Ford cars honking, beautiful bridges straddling the East River, the massive Empire State Building piercing the sky, friendly neighborhood cafes, baseball games in the park, walks along Coney Island's boardwalk, relaxing sidewalk strolls in the evenings and the city's ubiquitous love for music.

But all these places had now become like distant images far off on the horizons, where the Sun kissed the day goodnight.

***

Francis stood up from his rocking chair, stretched his arms above his head, and walked down to his small garden to water the flowers he'd planted in five rectangular vases. He stared at the old wooden fence that bordered his yard, hoping that Nikolla would come out to talk with him.

Thirty minutes passed before Francis finally had to accept that his buddy was not coming. With this realization, he walked toward the porch and sat down in the rocking chair once again. The Sun slowly went to rest for yet another night and the brilliant stars began to shimmer from far away in the dark blue sky.

Francis took two more sips from his beer bottle. He closed his eyes, rested his head against the back of the rocking chair, and imagined himself playing the cello again. He clearly imagined Tchaikovsky's Grand Adagio from Act II of Swan Lake. Its liltingly somber string melodies always evoked in him a deep sense of loneliness and melancholy.

Amidst all these feelings of sorrow, Francis enjoyed being alone because doing so helped him reflect on his past. He was uncertain whether his immediate family or close friends were still alive. To Francis, Brooklyn was his real home where he had spent a great deal of his childhood. His parents, Luke and Anna, were two Albanian emigres, who had provided him with an enjoyable and decent life with friends and family.

Francis had been a boy of many talents and therefore at a young age learned to play piano, cello, and baseball. When asked by adults which one he enjoyed the most, he'd always quickly answer: "All."

He had also fallen in love once, madly and deeply in love. Only that one time had he opened the fortified doors of his heart; unfortunately, since coming here he had to shut them tight due to pain and regret. He never seemed to get too close to any other women romantically - no matter how hard he tried. There was something missing from his past. What was missing was an impossible love, one that he would revisit only through the somber, sullen notes of music from his beloved cello.

***

He's now 47, old enough that he could've been married and have had a family. Instead, Francis had only grown old enough to be quite accustomed to a life alone.

He finished the beer, went inside the house, and turned on his bedroom light. From under an old Persian rug, Francis removed several planks from the wooden floor he had stained by hand. He reached down in a space under the floorboards with the frantic urgency of a parent rescuing their child from drowning.

From the dark space, he pulled out an old record player covered with years of dust and spiderwebs. It was the famous Gramophone Company brand, popular back when folks still called record players 'phonographs' or 'gramophones.' He had carried it with him since his days growing up back in Brooklyn.

He caressed the antique cover gently, closed his eyes for a moment, and imagined the beautiful music it had produced over the last thirty years. To Francis, it was not a mere old box. This was a magical box packed tight with feelings of mystery and memories of joy and pain. Yet, it was a box still carrying infinite possibilities. Filled with dreams that Francis would only dare to dream through the sound of its music.

After about a minute, Francis slowly lifted the cover. Unlike the old, dusty and stained exterior, the inside of this antique phonograph was in mint condition.

In many ways, Francis himself resembled this old phonograph. He too had grown older and somewhat gray on the exterior. But in his heart, filled with memories of his mystical past and magical love, he was graciously fresh and pure.

If Francis could turn back the hands of time and travel to his past, he would embrace love once again. He would go back precisely to the point in time when he held her in his arms next to the piano, beneath the bedroom sheets, or under the ancient oak tree.

After Francis finished tuning his old gramophone, he plugged it into the wall. Then he meticulously sifted through the old cardboard box, stained over the years with watermarks. He took out his favorite record and gently placed it on the turntable.

***

One hour passed. The music stopped.

Francis slowly stretched his arms to shake out their tingly numbness. He had listened to the kind of music considered taboo by rigid Communist Party standards. Jazz music, decadent and degenerate...

"Get rid of that damned box!" Nikolla told him two nights before. "Aren't you afraid someone might find out that you have a gramophone?"

"Afraid?" Francis had asked rhetorically.

"Well obviously, you must be afraid since you keep it underneath the rotten wood of your floor."

Nikolla was correct of course. Foreign music, like religious beliefs, had recently become forbidden in Albania, and Francis was wary that if too many people knew about his antique record player, he would become a target of ridicule, persecution, imprisonment. Recently, one of his former colleagues was taken away to prison for simply humming an Italian canzonet. Upon learning of this, Francis feverishly returned home that very night, cut several wooden pieces from the floor, and turned it into a secret hiding place for his magical box. Now he would only take it out when nostalgia for American music swept over him like a torrential hurricane.

"No one understands that when the gramophone plays, I can breathe again, live again." With that, Francis had put an end to all Nikolla's incessant questions.

He stood up from his rocking chair, imagining the gramophone playing his favorite tunes. Francis took a deep breath to replenish himself with the soft mist of the evening air. He raised his right arm high as if reaching for succulent summer grapes.

"Do you see that star?" Francis asked while pointing with his finger. "The one that burns the brightest."

"What about it?"

"Don't you see how beautifully it glows amid the darkness of the sky?"

"It is only a star!"

"No, it is not only a star. That is Lady Day. Simply, Lady Day."

"Lady who?" Nikolla asked now being completely lost in this suddenly mysterious conversation.

"It's a nickname for an American Blues singer. And a great singer, she was."

"Yeah, but just a singer, nonetheless..." Nikolla joked inadvertently.

"No, not just a singer," Francis insisted. "A singer like her, no Albanian has ever heard."

After making such a point, he remained silent and imagined the magically hypnotizing voice of Billie Holiday singing a song entitled, 'Strange Fruit.'

"Why do you amuse yourself with decadent music?" Nikolla insisted. "What do you hope to find in it?"

"Ghosts of my past!" Francis exclaimed. "I am sure Lady Day found ghosts of her past as well. She found love in music; she found you... she found me... she found all our loved ones... and all the broken people. God forgive me, but through that voice, I find great comfort during my many sleepless nights."

"Francis, your sleepless nights have gone on for twenty-eight years now," Nikolla had interrupted abruptly. "Why don't you let go of the ghosts? You're 47 now. Don't you want to build a family, a life?"

"It is too late for that."

"You're a fool!" Nikolla added. "That is precisely what you are."

Francis knew that Nikolla was correct once again. He could have built a comfortable life if only he had let go of the ghosts from his past. Perhaps he was too stubborn, or maybe dissatisfied with the path his life had followed. It was true he loved everything about this picturesque town, the warm characteristics of the houses and the welcoming old taverns. The locals had loved him in return; they considered him to be kind and gentle, soft-spoken and poetic. Kids spoke warmly to their parents about him. He had become a fatherly figure to all the town's children, a role model.

The women in town saw him as a lost romantic. Long ago, he had played the cello in closed performances. They simply marveled at the sight of him gliding the bow over the strings. The music was something extraordinarily beautiful that struck them deeply. For them, his sense of great passion and emotional intensity was immeasurable –

perhaps even otherworldly.

Back in the capital city of Tirana, he had become an instant favorite with the Party's elites. For six magical years, members of the top political echelon had rushed to claim him as a great product of the proletariat. In his mind, he was more a product of his deep love for music. So, to diplomatically avoid a life filled more with political intrigue than with music lovers, he requested to be deployed to the south, where he could better serve young people.

People from Tirana still remembered him though. Not long ago, Francis walked into the principal's office to find him talking with a man peculiarly dressed all in black. "I heard you play in Tirana at the National Gallery of Arts during your last performance in 1962," the man bellowed. Then he turned to the principal and continued: "This man here can make a cello cry."

Francis clearly understood the notoriety and life of privilege he had given up by moving here. But he could not allow his name and music to be used for political purposes. Now, he only played the cello sporadically. Behind closed curtains. At nighttime.

It was during one of those nights that he met Nina, a beautiful local woman who immediately marveled at the way he poured all his emotions, pain, and nostalgia over the cello strings. She had gone as far as proclaiming Francis 'an Albanian Mozart.'

Nina briefly interested Francis. Unlike many of the other local women, she had long and wavy blonde hair, emerald, blue eyes, and a sweet voice. Francis was instantly drawn to her.

She too had been drawn to Francis. His dark brown eyes gave her the impression that he had hidden passions longing to erupt like a volcano.

They became closer over the course of the next ten months. They would talk about life, beauty, and love in general terms. Then they would spend romantic nights walking along the rocky shores. Occasionally, they would stop to make passionate love while the coastal waves caressed their bodies. However, that all ended one day when they decided to visit a picturesque site along the road on the outskirts of Saranda.

***

Francis and Nina walked along a small road that led to the scenic clearing rich with nature's beauty. They deftly navigated around a scattering of mudholes. The soil was still quite soft and wet because of the heavy rain the previous night. From the clearing, they could see a magnificently radiant halo of sunlight cast over the hills in the distance. The hills, lying under a crystal clear, cloudless sky, was blanketed with orange trees and silvery-green olive groves.

Minutes after continuing along the road they made a final turn. Both stood frozen with amazement as if they were seeing it for the first time. There was the Blue Eye on a beautiful afternoon, a little over twelve miles north of Saranda.

The ancient site had gotten its name because the source of Bistrica River resembled a gigantic eye. At its center, the eye was formed from the deep blue underground springs that naturally ascended the river in a circular motion. Around the edges, the eye was framed with turquoise blue waters of the river and shaded with ancient oak trees.

Nina invited him to sit beneath one of the timeless oak trees. From her brown leather bag, she pulled out a gourd-shaped bottle and handed it to Francis. The Sun blazed on his head and the sweat drops stung his eyes. After Francis wiped the sweat from his sleeve, he poured cool water on his head and sat soaking beneath the oak tree.

After his gourd had no more water, Francis refilled it from the icy-cold waters of the pristine river and handed it back to Nina.

"There you go."

"I'm not thirsty now," she replied with a soft smile.

"Well, put it in your bag," he instructed her with a scolding tone. "We may need it on the way back into town"

It was the first time she'd seen him get agitated. Nina quickly stood up and walked to the river's edge. She bent down and slowly ran her fingers through the flowing, crystal-clear water. The coldness of the river sent chills through her body. She abruptly stood up and turned to look at Francis and said, "Make a wish!"

"Excuse me?" Francis stood there frozen in place, as if distraught by the ghosts of his past, ghosts that had finally awakened and wrestled in front of his eyes.

He suddenly remembered, long ago in 1941, that exact phrase being said in this precise place; although then, those words had come from the tongue of the love of his life, the one person whom he could never forget. Francis thought his memory of her would have faded away completely with the passage of time. At the very least, he tried not to think of her as often. "My wish is to be with you forever and ever," he had vowed that warm summer evening back in 1941.

Now Francis sat still and quiet as the grave. His previously agitated visage now transformed into a sullenly stoic expression. Nina, confused and concerned, stood in front of him aghast.

"Nina, please, come sit here beside me. There's a story I would like to tell you."

They sat there beside the flowing waters for three hours as Francis confided everything to her about his life back in Brooklyn. He told her about how he'd loved once with every ounce of his being and how fate had dealt a bitter blow to his young two-year love affair. Upon conclusion of his tale, Francis rested his head against the trunk of the timelessly sturdy oak tree and once again sat in contemplative silence.

She began weeping. Nina did not quite understand whether she was crying because she felt such horrible sorrow for Francis' loss or because she had suddenly realized she'd always been his second greatest love. Whichever the cause for her tears, that day they came to the mutual understanding that it was for the best to stop seeing each other.

***

Francis had wanted to be gentler with Nina during their time at the Blue Eye. Her past had been full of sad memories as well. She too had once loved with all her heart before meeting Francis. Nina had fallen in love, as a young woman, with an Albanian man from an impoverished family. When her mother realized that their relationship was getting serious, she ordered her daughter to immediately stop seeing him. Suspiciously, at this exact time, Nina's boyfriend abruptly left town without offering a reason or leaving a break-up letter.

Severely depressed, Nina tried asking others in the village for help in dealing with all her emotions. Of course, she was unsuccessful getting help because of the realities of living in a small village. In this village, as in all small towns and villages all over the world, people had plenty of time on their hands and spent it enjoying any town gossip. Therefore, all Nina could do was devote the years, following her traumatic breakup, attempting to overcome her deep emotional scars.

Francis was genuinely considerate of her pain from her breakup with her first love. He certainly did not want to end their relationship so abruptly while they were standing beneath the ancient oak tree. Francis had deep feelings for Nina but could not understand why he saw the face of another woman when asked to make a wish. The face of a love long gone.

He sat near the window, put his hands together, lifted his arms over his head, and then rested his head on the palms of his hands. Francis closed his eyes and began to lose himself in all the memories that came to dominate his life over the years.

"I'll be seeing you

In all the old familiar places

That this heart of mine embraces

All day through..."

Francis enjoyed sitting here at nighttime, especially after a long day at the school, letting his thoughts travel thousands of miles away. He deeply missed Brooklyn where he spent the first nineteen years of his life. The cavernous movie theaters, summertime fireworks, baseball games, Yankees' ticker-tape parades, summer camps, and the gorgeous teenage girls of New York City were all permanently seared into his memory. A memory of a time long ago and of distant places thousands of miles across the vast Atlantic Ocean.

What Francis remembered most vividly about New York City was the day he took the subway to the Bronx and heard the great Lou Gehrig make his famous farewell speech at Yankee Stadium. It was the day that changed his life forever.

A Cellist and the Swan

Tuesday, the Fourth of July 1939. A gorgeously clear blue sky blanketed Yankee Stadium in The Bronx as more than 61,000 applauding spectators looked on as an esteemed former baseball player, once named 'the iron man' for his athletic perseverance, approached a lone microphone stand in centerfield. He walked slow and deliberate with his head down while struggling to hold back his tears. When the applause finally died down, the entire world of baseball seemed to momentarily hold its collective breath and listened to his clear and resounding voice humbly thanking them all for their support.

Francis had arrived at Yankee Stadium early that morning. There was a doubleheader scheduled. No pre-game batting practice. Today, this entire pre-game period belonged to Lou Gehrig. Francis watched with great sadness and sorrow as his hero bid farewell to baseball. So deep was his admiration for the 'iron horse' that he had learned to emulate his disciplined work ethic, dedication to the game of baseball, and his batting stance.

Francis had grown to love every aspect of the game. He loved the smells of the freshly cut grass and rich soil on the baseball diamond, the sight of white foul poles leaning in the warm breeze as the players' cleats scratch and dig into the basepaths, the snug fit of the baseball mitt, the sound of the ball's contact with the bat during batting practice, and the refreshing, thirst-quenching taste of water from the water fountains.

Often, he would discuss facets of the game with his friend Jonathan Bianchi, who was three years his senior. They first met when Jonathan was an umpire at a baseball game in Bensonhurst. During his first at-bat, Francis dug his cleats into the ground in the batter's box which left dirt all over home plate. Then he used a tight swing while holding the bat near the knob, to unleash a screaming double. During his second appearance at the plate, Francis had hit a single straight down the middle, driving home two runs from players on second and third bases. Again, he had dug his feet into the ground, leaving another pile of dirt all over home plate. Francis' elaborate grinding of his cleats had not sat well with Jonathan who then called Francis out on strikes during his third at-bat.

"That's a ball," Francis angrily protested.

"Next time, don't get my home plate dirty," Jonathan grinned.

Over the next two years, they became close friends.

Jonathan was the oldest brother of Kansas, one of Francis' classmates. She and Francis had been good friends ever since elementary school. One day, however, she accidentally spilled the beans and told everyone in class that Francis liked Celeste Salek, her new friend from Boston.

Francis was extremely embarrassed by the incident. The other children at school began teasing him and so, he blamed Kansas. Since then, they sort of grew distant from each other. Only when he became good friends with Jonathan, had Francis decided to bury the hatchet and accept Kansas back into his life.

Francis left the doubleheader early, so he could meet up with the two of them. They had made plans to drive into the heart of Astoria that evening and watch a ballet performance at a fundraising gala.

From the start, Johnny hated the entire idea of going to the performance. According to him, ballet was not something men should watch. "It's too much to bear!" he had exclaimed. Francis, on the other hand, did not mind it one bit and had been looking forward to it. "You're in for a great surprise," Kansas told him.

There was another reason that Francis wanted to go, he had a deep appreciation for, and emotional connection with, music and the performing arts. He came from a large family of artists and performers, who always motivated and encouraged each other to become better at their respective art forms. His mother had been the most influential person in his life by instilling in him a passion for the piano. "His fingers are long and thin," one of the musician relatives had once told her. "Perfect hands for a pianist." So Francis' mother made sure that he dedicated himself to countless hours of practice. Along the way, his love for music broadened to include a passion for another instrument. He developed a love for the cello. Francis believed the key to his talent on the cello was the softness of his hands, which enabled him to play with a uniquely relentless vigor emoting his inner passion.

The fundraiser was held at the spacious Bohemian Hall in Queens. It was a gathering place for Czech and Slovak expats who had fled the ironfisted rule of the Austro-Hungarian Empire during the latter half of the nineteenth century. The property on which the building sat was adjoined to a garden where many people would gather during warm summer nights. They would drink beer varieties while sitting at communal picnic tables and socialize with their neighbors.

But on this night, the garden would serve a different purpose than those other evenings. It had transformed into a place catering to children of those wealthy people who were willing to dip into their wallets and hand out large sums of money. The proceeds from the fundraiser were to help recent Czech immigrants, who had fled Nazi-occupied Czechoslovakia, to start a new life in the 'Promised Land' of America.

There were about eighty or ninety elegantly dressed guests. They stood throughout the Hall, clustered into several small groups eagerly chatting with each other about various topics. "I had to travel all the way to New Jersey to buy this dress," said a dainty young woman showing off her flowing black dress. "I have been anxiously awaiting this performance for weeks," said a well-dressed gentleman in another group.

"The Carnival of the Animals," Francis eagerly read from a poster on a nearby wall as he walked through the main hall. "Fund Raising Gala!"

"How are we allowed in here if we have no money to give?" he nervously asked Kansas with a deeply worried look on his face.

"We have special invitations," Jonathan replied as he smirked at Francis.

The three of them sat at a table close to the main stage. Francis looked around at the hypnotic way the lights reflected off the instruments and illuminated the wooden stage. Behind a podium at stage right, the orchestra's conductor was busily shuffling through several sheets of music. They looked on in delight as a flutist, a clarinetist; two pianists, a xylophonist, two violinists, a cellist, and a double bass player individually practiced their pieces and warmed their instruments. The musical notes playing all at once created a chaotically cacophonous mixture of sounds.

Even at this young age, Francis greatly admired anyone who had the courage to perform in front of large audiences. "It must be an overwhelming experience to face hundreds of spectators and still be able to convey and evoke deep emotions through flawless performances," he often thought.

Suddenly, he remembered Lou Gehrig's emotional speech earlier in the afternoon. Gehrig had bid farewell to the sport he adored and cherished. Although the speech was not a performance by any stretch of the imagination, his words nonetheless had been a heartfelt display of tears and emotions on the largest stage of all - that of Yankee Stadium.

"What had it been like for the iron horse to say goodbye to the game he loved so deeply?" Francis imagined.

Suddenly, the conductor loudly tapped his baton on the wooden podium, signaling the start of the performance and abruptly bringing Francis' thoughts back to the present. The musicians quickly readied themselves.

Then a moment of pregnant silence…

The conductor raised his right arm gently in the air. One, two, three…

The introductory movement began with the orchestral piano playing a bold tremolo, under which the strings entered with the piece's powerful theme. The theme was called "The March of The Lion" and it evoked the strength of the most powerful of all animals. The music expressed the lion's majesty as he marched fearlessly through the jungle while all the other animals cautiously watched and moved aside. A fearless conqueror, the undisputed king.

The next twelve movements went quickly, a virtue that could only be attributed to a well-coordinated orchestra. Kansas, sensing Francis' enjoyment of the show so far, turned to him and whispered, "The best is yet to come."

After the twelfth piece ended, the stage lights went off and there was a moment of silence in the darkened hall. Suddenly, a projector from the back of the room cast a bright spotlight in the direction of the cellist. He began to gently glide the bow stick against the strings of the cello as if mesmerized by the light itself. Soon, the piano joined in softly to the melody.

Just then, another spotlight illuminated the left corner of the stage. From behind the curtain, a graceful ballerina slowly appeared dressed all in white. She instantly captivated the audience with her beauty. She was tall and slender, with a long swan-like neck, high angular cheekbones, and hair neatly tied in a ponytail.

She gracefully waved her arms through the air in a flawlessly gentle motion, evoking a swan's wings as it swims across the lake. Perfectly emulating a swan's legs beneath the surface of the water, she tip-toed across the stage appearing to magically float across toward the audience.

Suddenly, a dramatic shift…

The ballerina began to tragically flail her arms through the air as if something strange was happening. The audience watched as the swan fluttered her wings grotesquely, unable to continue her once peaceful journey across the calm waters.

And then… amidst these panicked motions, the swan's erratic movement was overtaken once again by its flowingly peaceful outstretched wings. The elegant ballerina sunk slowly onto her left knee; her right leg stretched forward - flat on the floor. She brought her right arm slowly over her leg, resting her delicate head on her right hand. Motionless wings… Unmoving legs... The swan had lain to rest.

The audience erupted with feverish applause while giving an enthusiastic standing ovation. The ballerina bowed forward graciously. For a moment, she looked directly at Francis and smiled at him. Kansas shouted over the loud cheers of the audience: "Wasn't she fantastic!" Francis was speechless… still completely captivated by the beautiful swan.

After the rapturous grand finale, Jonathan and Kansas navigated through the throngs of the crowd. Francis remained seated. He stared, frozen with awe towards the stage, a pleasantly disbelieving witness to a spectacular dance.

He completely blocked out the sound of the crowd for the next five or ten minutes. He vividly imagined the dying swan, the gentle movement, and its sudden sporadic flutter, these two contradictions set against the achingly somber melody of the cello.

While enraptured by the image, Francis suddenly had a clear and profound epiphany. He promptly stood up from the table and looked around as if something were trying to chase him. At that instant, he noticed Jonathan and Kansas approaching with the ballerina. She had now changed into a red and white polka dotted dress. Francis almost immediately felt a lump in his throat as he nervously watched her approach. However, he quickly tried to gather his pose with a smile.

"Hi, I am Francis. Pleasure to meet you," he greeted with feigned confidence while extending his right hand.

"The pleasure is mine, Francis Petrela!" the ballerina replied with a warm smile and shook his hand.

"You've dug up my last name from reliable sources I see," he chuckled nervously, suspiciously glaring in Kansas' and Johnny's direction.

"It's a small world it seems," she giggled. "And the world has ears!"

"Believe what you want though," the ballerina continued. "But I still remember how you comforted me when I fell off the bike."

"Oh my God!" he muttered. "Celeste?" He looked down, suddenly feeling yet another lump in his throat. Although, this time accompanied by a dry mouth and sweaty palms. His eyes bulged in extreme surprise and his strong emotions resurfaced...

Francis tried desperately to collect himself. He smiled while closely examining every inch of her face. He did not mind one bit the way that she had suddenly rushed into his life like an uncontrollably, blazing fire.

How could he mind? He mapped out every inch of her beauty in his mind. Those dreamy hazel eyes, cute thin nose, beautifully delicate cheekbones, luscious rosy lips, snowy white skin, and a beauty birthmark right beneath the bottom lip... There stood a girl who now had grown stunningly more beautiful over the years.

Francis moved aside and invited her to sit while his heart beat through his chest with a force he had never experienced before.

Francis had secretly admired Celeste when they were both eleven. They had never expressed any romantic feelings or emotional displays though. They never even spent time alone, except when Kansas would momentarily separate from them to get ice cream. They were only innocent kids back then. And at best, his feelings for her only could be detected by the feeling of butterflies in his stomach every time he'd see her.

All four of them walked over to the nearest empty table. Francis made sure to sit next to Celeste, while Jonathan and Kansas sat across from them. Throughout the evening, Jonathan was the center of the conversation and did most of the talking. As always, he entertained the group with his typical flamboyantly arrogant manner and recounted colorfully descriptive stories that kept them all laughing.

Francis would occasionally sneak a peek at Celeste out of the corner of his eye. "…but none of these can top the look on Francis' face when I called him out on strikes," Jonathan boisterously concluded.

Francis embarrassingly glared at Johnny for a few seconds, shook his head in disbelief, and smirked. "God forbid someone gets your precious home plate dirty." Then, all four of them broke out into laughter.

"So, I hear you like baseball," Celeste said suddenly shifting everyone's attention on Francis.

In that very instance, he turned to her and was dumbstruck with how beautiful her hazel eyes were under the lights.

"Yes, baseball is a game I play to have an enjoyable time," Francis replied in an uncharacteristically low tone.

Celeste smiled and nodded in approval. "Well, the game seems to have many facets, which do you like best?"

Francis looked at the floor for a moment to collect his thoughts and make sure he correctly understood the question. Few people he knew showed any interest in the details of baseball, and so Francis had never really prepared for the kind of intelligently considered answer that her question required.

"Well, the game depends on the interdependence of all its elements; a lot of things must go right for a team to win. A team's victory is often a balanced combination of a well-pitched game, a great defense in the outfield, an infield hit, a sac bunt or maybe a hit and run, a stolen base, a powerful home run, a sacrifice fly, and then there goes another win. But if I really had to pick only one aspect that I like the most, then I'd have to say it's teamwork." He smiled and exhaled loudly, satisfied and relieved with his well thought out and articulated answer.

Now Francis was much less nervous and more emotionally collected. His once nervously halting voice was now confidently smooth, calm, and articulate. Perhaps, he had never needed to prepare for an elaborately intelligent answer when it came to baseball. Discussing the game of baseball was such a comfortable topic for him that he always sounded like a genuine student of the game, with knowledgeable insights into all its aspects.

Celeste, intrigued by his obvious passion for baseball, looked him deep in the eyes. "Your eyes seem so mysterious!" she thought. She vividly remembered those same chestnut brown eyes when she'd fallen off her bike years ago. "It's only a little bruise," Francis said to her as she gazed into those caring eyes then, the same way she stared at them now. "This is not happening," she thought in total disbelief of the groundswell of affection, she suddenly felt.

"Would you like to take a walk?" Francis leaned toward her and whispered in her ear. When she felt the warmth of his breath against her ear, Celeste's entire body felt electric.

Celeste looked at him, grabbed the tablecloth on her lap and twirled it nervously. She nodded her head in approval.

"We're going for a walk," she muttered, her eyes quickly shifting back and forth between Jonathan and Kansas.

***

The night was dark, and the streets were silent. The two and three-storied semi-detached houses lay along a good length of Twenty-Fourth Avenue as Francis and Celeste walked carelessly down the sidewalk, beneath the starry sky, and through the soft midnight breeze. There were some scattered Ford cars parked along the tree-lined street. Francis stopped for one moment and glanced at the sky, where the gentle moonlight had turned clouds silver. As he turned to Celeste, he asked with a soft and deep voice, "Do you hear that?"

They stood there as Fourth of July firecrackers exploded in the distance somewhere over Manhattan. Then, as the loud sounds momentarily stopped, they looked at each other and listened to the silence, both realizing how nights like these were genuine and rare. These sorts of nights were genuine because they had special meaning for these two honest, innocent, and hopefully optimistic 16 year-olds. Young people untainted by life's hypocrisy, willing to openly reveal their own shy vulnerability to each other, and yet brave enough, on this night, to reach out to one another's hearts in hopes of finding love. Nights like these, where two souls find one another, were also rare because of the way Francis and Celeste had been instantly drawn to each other, moments before.

As they looked into each other's eyes, Celeste's face reddened, and she quickly lowered her eyes. He smiled but turned and started walking away as if he were afraid that she might feel trapped by the power of his eyes.

After forcefully regaining her emotional composure, she began to walk faster to catch up to him. After they again walked in tandem, Celeste broke the heavy silence. "Besides baseball, what else do you do?"

"I like to read, listen to music, watch Fred Astaire and Ginger Rogers dance in their movies," he paused for a moment. "Go for long rides on the subway to think."

"Think?" She asked. In that instance, she wondered whether Francis had ever thought about her in all those years after they had stopped their quick trips to the amusement park.

"Yes, think," he replied convincingly.

"What is it that you think about?" she asked, now quite eager to learn much more about him.

"I don't know… different stuff. I think about life, about what I want to do in the future. Sometimes, I'll be confused about things, but then I play the piano. Then, suddenly all my thoughts become clear, and my problems seem less difficult to solve."

"Do you really play the piano?"

"Yes, why do you ask?" Francis asked puzzlingly.

"I'm impressed. I didn't expect someone our age to have such a thorough appreciation for music. I mean you don't play the piano for money or fame, but because you feel compelled to the sounds of the music itself. To me, that is amazing!"

Celeste continued to walk next to him, smiling inside and thinking, "You're an angel Francis or even a saint. Saint Francis more precisely."

As they walked side by side through the gentle breeze of the night, Francis felt an urge to tell her that he also played the cello. However, he did not want to dominate the whole conversation by talking about himself the whole time. She might think that he was showing off and self-centered.

"What about you? What do you do with your time?" he asked.

"I ride my bike most evenings. Sometimes, I hang out with friends and go to the movies. Though, most of my time is spent on school and learning. It is a little tough for me because both of my parents expect the world of me academically. My mom wants me to become either a doctor or a lawyer. My father is a little bit more lenient though."

"You dance beautifully," Francis said.

Celeste said nothing. During the past couple of years, she had relentlessly practiced, despite, her parents showing contempt for it. They could not understand her love for ballet. They had other ideas for her future. "You have to learn so you can have a real profession," her mother would always say scoldingly.

"What do you enjoy the most?" Francis asked intently.

Celeste's great love for ballet and this romantic night walk with Francis combined to gift her with an overwhelmingly inexplicable feeling. She suddenly stopped walking and turned to face him and look directly into his eyes as he walked forward.

"I dance to the music that you play," she answered with a soft, sweet, and innocent voice.

He nearly stumbled as he heard the words and took a step back involuntarily. "I dance to the music that you play," the words sweetly resonated in his heart more than any musical note he had ever played. Those words were so suddenly spoken yet so innocently sincere and heartfelt. Francis turned around and gazed at Celeste from five yards away.

She was shining beautifully in the moonlight's glow. The gentle summer breeze softly caressed her long brown hair. He looked deep into her hazel eyes, shining with flecks of moonlight, and drank in the totality of her sincerity, softness, and beauty.

He felt another lump swelling in his throat, similar to the one that he had experienced earlier in the evening. Francis stepped to her, futilely fighting back his nerves. He gently took her hands, laid them close to his chest, and asked her to close her eyes.

"Can you dance to this music?"

She felt his heart pounding. Tick, tick, tick… Its beats, increased in tempo, as her hand remained atop the most precious gift of life, the heart itself. And then she understood how nervous Francis must have been, for she felt the same way. Celeste had never been able to connect with anyone so deeply. For her, this deep connection was all new.

Francis had to be sent from heaven. She wished she could have realized it when they were both eleven. But again, she was a child back then. What did she know? Regardless, she's glad that it was him now, and nobody else, walking with her at midnight.

Ironically, this midnight walk under the starry sky was not supposed to be a date. Nor was the night intended to evolve into an enjoyable combination of serious talk, romantic emotions, and nervous passion.

As midnight approached and firecrackers continued exploding in the starry, dark blue sky over Manhattan, Francis and Celeste walked together in the streets of Astoria. In the distance, they heard sporadic sounds of thunder. The coastal clouds began to intensify in the sky as they heard and smelled the first raindrops kiss the warm pavement where they stood.

The two remained unfazed, unmoved. The smell of the rain combined with the green summer leaves and the rich soil on the ground added its own sensory delight to this significant moment. And as the rain intensified, they both held and hugged each other. They kissed passionately under the silvery sky. From that night on, they became inseparable.

Back to 1969: The Lamp Light

Francis opened the door. Outside it was pitch black as the sources of distant sounds of nature, although faintly muffled, hid behind the enveloping darkness of the night.

With the slight illumination of moonlight, Francis moved slowly to the left, right outside the front door. After lighting the wick, he lifted the lantern from the rusted hook that was attached to the wooden pillar.

Then he carefully walked down the small porch steps and made his way towards the stone well in the middle of the yard. Francis held the lamp high enough to light his pathway. He hung the lamp on the vertical beams which held the wooden hand-cranked wheel. The flame barely lit the inside of the brick-lined walls of the well. Slowly, he lowered the bucket, by the attached rope, down into the deep, enclosed shaft.

After drawing fresh, chilly water from the well, Francis untied the bucket from the rope, lifted it loose from any entanglements, and paused to look up. The sky was silver now with the moon hidden halfway behind a cluster of rolling clouds. His knees had been hurting earlier in the day, a reliably recurring signal to him of imminent rain. He did not mind the pain. He would bear his aching knees for the gift of rain at any time. The last time it rained, the northern part of the river had completely burst its banks and now, not even a month later, the nearby creeks had started to dry up. Francis knew it was only a matter of time before the well would begin to run low.

He breathed in deeply, allowing the fresh, cool night's air to fill his lungs. Things now seemed so tranquil as the world's hectic sounds and movements came to a halt. And in that moment, Francis was reminded of what made this place so uncharacteristically natural and beautiful.

He set the bucket beside his feet and got down on his knees. He knelt there, enveloped in both the heavenly light of the moon and his small lantern's flame, still affixed to the wooden pillar. Francis stuck his thumb in the soft soil. He glided his thumb across the dirt and slowly spelled out some incomprehensible patterns. This particular set of patterns were immensely meaningful to him in the grand scheme of what was going on in his life – however confusingly it might have appeared to a watching bystander. Only he understood the special meaning of the musical notes from Camille Saint-Saens. It was one of those solitary acts that defied human logic but made perfect sense in nature, beyond man's reason.

He stood up, picked up the bucket, and slowly returned with it to the old house. In the darkness, one could easily confuse him with a homeless tramp, who had wandered his entire life in search of something of hidden value. A concept that is incomprehensible to most people and understood only to those who have ever dared to dream or been fearless enough to hold on to the most indispensable aspects of life.

Immediately after locking the front door behind him, Francis poured water from the bucket into a basin that was sitting on the hallway floor. He wiped his hands on his pants. Chills suddenly shivered down his spine. The weather was becoming a little cooler now, prompting him to tightly wrap an old throw blanket over his shoulders. He sat beside the window with a glass of fresh water sitting on the table in front of him. His lips were parched, and the fresh water would undoubtedly quench his thirst.

Through the window, Francis could see the lantern hanging over the well outside. It was casting a warm light encircling the area around the well. He watched as the small flame burn slowly through the night. The lantern's flame remained defiantly lit, despite the encroaching darkness. The sight of this evoked strong inspirational feelings in him. Greatly moved by watching the flame's steadfastness, Francis grabbed the pen and paper, which had been sitting unused on the table for more than a month.

My Dearest Love,

In life, there is a time when each one of us realizes our own personal obsessions that burn our very being with a fire of hope and desire. This tiny flickering flame can withstand all the turbulent winds of life and never be extinguished. Its warmth unequivocally provides us all the small spark necessary for our spiritual survival.

Such a flame can only persist through our own stubborn determination to follow our heart's desires. This fire of hope and desire only shines brightest when each of us has finally obtained the object of our desire. If it were not for that tiny flickering flame, we might as well surrender to hopelessness and despair, for a person without hope or desire is devoid of life itself.

You, my dear, are the reason why this flame inside me can never be snuffed out. Its warmth enables me to move forward in my life. To continue to *hope and desire all the things that I might have forgotten without it. I know I can go on into storms of life. For I know that you are the reason I still exist. Even when I am at my lowest, I do not feel lost or forgotten for this flame warms my dampened soul and its light brightens the dark night of my despair.*

Francis placed the pencil down on the desk and watched the flame of the lamp once again. He had swallowed hard moments ago, wanting desperately to quench the thirst inside him. But there were certain things that can never be extinguished. And one thing was certain. There was a little fire burning inside him, which no water, no creek, and no river could ever quench.

The flame that burned slowly inside of him eventually led him again to his beloved record player. The record that caught his eye was Beethoven's Piano Sonata No. 14. He placed the record on the record player and then its "Moonlight Sonata" began playing. His favorite moment, a duet between the piano and cello always grabbed his heart and possessed his soul.

The blanket draped over Francis' shoulders now had become a characteristic prop for the tramp, the wanderer, the explorer of indefinite ideas.

He soon laid down and closed his eyes.

He fondly remembered every detail that ensued after their first night.

***

First, Celeste began to go to every one of his baseball games. She would get such a kick out of watching him grind his cleats into the dirt on the field. Francis would assume his batting stance at home plate and,

BAM! He'd unleash a screaming double straight down the line. After he'd reached second base, he would look at Celeste cheering in the stands, and point at her as if saying, "This one was for you, beautiful!" Whenever Francis would steal a base or hustle down the base paths, Celeste would hold her breath hoping he would not get hurt. Then he would turn to her with a painful grimace hidden beneath his smile as if saying, "This one was for you again!"

When the baseball games ended, Celeste would always run to Francis and jump on him while hugging him tight and kissing him. Their passionate embrace looked as if they hadn't seen each other in years. "You're funny... I adore you," she would always say.

Then, he took her to his house. Although the outside did not have much glamour or seem particularly different than the rest of the block, the house had quite an extraordinary interior. It had been rebuilt through his father's keen eye for decorating details. While showing her his two-storied home, Francis told her that he had been named after Sir Francis Bacon, a renowned English philosopher, statesman, and essayist. "His main goal in life was to discover the truth," Francis said. Celeste had been increasingly falling in love with Francis during their brief reacquaintance. Now she wondered if he, like Francis Bacon, had discovered a different type of truth. Her love for him. "All this time I kept thinking you were named after Saint Francis of Assisi," she said teasingly laughing. One day, in his study room at home, he played Fred Astaire's "Cheek to Cheek" on the piano for her. That's when they made love for the first time. On the floor beside the piano.

When school started in the fall, they were not able to spend as much time together. But they spent every other evening going to the movies, visiting the Coney Island Amusement Park on the boardwalk in Brooklyn, riding their bicycles, or walking down Astoria Park overlooking the shores of the East River.

Francis and Celeste also spent many evenings at a tiny coffee shop on Broadway in Astoria. They went there to sit, relax, and eat ice creams or drink milkshakes. They had done so all through the summer and now had become frequent visitors. Celeste wrote a short essay about the café when her English professor, in mid-September, instructed the class to describe their favorite place.

She rewrote a copy of the essay on high-quality bond-type paper, slightly perfumed with her favorite scent, and gave it to Francis. Celeste told him he should read it and smell it any time they might get into any type of arguments in the future.

Francis then playfully reciprocated by writing tons of short notes and secretly slipping them into her pockets. The notes read things like, "Just so you won't forget me tomorrow" or "Dance to my music."

***

Her 17th birthday in 1939 was probably the most pleasant surprise. Francis had a tall grandfather clock in his house which he had jokingly named 'Big Ben.' A few days before Celeste's birthday Francis set the clock to wake him up by chiming loudly at the top of every hour. Each time it chimed, he would wake up, contemplate the best conceivable way to surprise her and fall back asleep. He finally decided he would take her that night to the Hudson River. When they got there, he asked her to close her eyes and began playing the cello for her under the moonlight. "Oh my god," she gasped suddenly, "a familiar sound."

She could not believe what she was hearing, so she opened her eyes. At first, Celeste could only see his outline in front of his Ford's headlights. Francis remained seated on the edge of a bench as he played his cello, placed upright between his legs. Celeste stared in confusion while listening to the beautiful notes. She did not know how to react. This was all too sudden. She knew he played the piano. He liked to dig his cleats in the dirt while playing baseball; she knew that too. But she never anticipated this. The cello and "The Dying Swan." Francis had kept them both secret from her. Now she was torn between whether to love him or hate him for his secrecy.

***

The morning was still young, and the Sun had barely begun to graze the sky. Everything seemed fresh and beautiful. The dew covered the cool, green blades of grass. Fallen Autumn leaves rustled beneath their feet. They stayed there passionately embracing and kissing like two lovers who longed desperately to connect with each other in every possible form. In life and in the afterlife. Longing that they would never have to separate. This would be their perfect scenario, an impossibly romantic notion that one would find on the front of a wedding card.

The following day, Celeste organized a birthday party at her home. Friends and relatives started arriving at seven o'clock in the evening. She danced with Francis to the hypnotic voice of Billie Holiday. After everyone had left, Francis and Celeste walked through the street that ran along the East River. The sky was clear and the air heavy with humidity. As they crossed beneath the Triborough Bridge, Francis stopped, turned to Celeste, and asked her to close her eyes. Then he walked behind her, took out a silver necklace and placed it gently around her neck. She opened her eyes.

The delicate necklace did not catch her eye or gleam brightly, but she noticed its attached heart-shaped locket. "What's in there," she asked. "Look for yourself," he playfully responded. Celeste opened the locket and saw a tiny, folded piece of paper. She carefully unfolded the paper and read aloud, "Just so you won't forget me tomorrow." She impulsively threw her arms around him and rested her head on his chest. They held each other tightly, both understanding that overnight their love had skyrocketed to a whole different level.

***

A year later, Francis went over to Celeste's home to have dinner with her parents. In keeping with old Albanian customs, he'd brought a platter of stuffed eggplants his grandmother had made for them. Though Celeste's mother, Lynn, was skeptical initially of them dating at such a youthful age, Francis had been able to win over both parents with his maturity and careful words. Additionally, he had recently been accepted to Columbia University. So, Lynn had begun to appreciate such a fine, upstanding young man like him for her daughter.

After dinner, Francis and Celeste went out on the porch. There they remained very sullen and quiet. For a few moments, Celeste stared at the heart-shaped locket, languidly hanging above her breasts. She picked up the locket and kissed it while the summer breeze ran through her soft hair. Then she looked up to the sky and pointed, "You see Francis? You see that star?"

"Which one?"

Up to that point, Francis had been paying more attention to her supple neckline while she was looking at the sky. God, she is beautiful, he thought. Engrossingly occupied by the gleaming constellations of stars, she did not notice how his eyes lovingly followed her every move.

"The one that burns the brightest," Celeste innocently replied.

"Oh yeah, I see it," Francis responded while still looking at her under the starlit sky. He knew that the brightest star that night was standing right in front of him.

"That is Lady Day," said Celeste. Then, with a warm, broad smile, she turned her head slightly toward Francis and their eyes met. With a sweet, soft voice, she asked, "Baby, do you want to dance?"

"With no music?"

"Just follow my lead," she reassured him.

Now the night was dark with crickets loudly chirping somewhere off in the distance. Their only light came from her porch lamp and the innumerable stars in the endless sky. The slight summer breeze suddenly stopped and made the warm, heavy air eerily still. Yet they danced without any music. They danced to the simplest, most precious music of all. The beat of their two loving hearts.

Back to 1969: The Near Impossible

Now it was twenty minutes past eleven at night. With the old blanket still hung over his shoulders, Francis sat on the edge of the bed, in a lonely room where darkness dominated every miserable corner. Memories flooded his mind and overwhelmed him with feelings of fear and terror. Although he had experienced these feelings many times before, he again became frozen like it was happening to him for the first time.

Salty tears poured down from the corners of his deep brown eyes as if attempting to wash away the last twenty-eight years. But no matter how hard or how often his tears poured from his swollen eyes, they could never seem to wash away his memories of the love he used to have. Though optimism, happiness, innocence, and hope had all been far removed from his reality, the memories of these emotions were still vivid in his mind and relentlessly tormented him especially in dark moments like these.

Over the years, the endless torrent of tears had stopped and instead become a simple drizzle imbued with idealistic notions and bygone memories. Francis had tried futilely to forget the past. Perhaps he had briefly been successful at one point or another. It had been in his best interest to attempt to do so.

But on this night, he couldn't submerge his pent-up feelings. During this one evening, the past had come hurling towards him like a storm. All Francis could do now was sit in emotional pain and agony, not knowing what to do next, not knowing how to dispel his unimaginable torment.

Over the last three decades, Francis had waited for what fate would bring him in the next twenty-eight minutes, twenty-eight hours, twenty-eight days, twenty-eight weeks, twenty-eight months, twenty-eight years. Or perhaps he'd waited too long for what fate would instead bring in the next twenty-eight lifetimes.

Joyous memories, Bohemian Hall, the Café, their bicycle rides, intimate moments, their undisputable love, had helped settle his mind over the years and ameliorate his sense of loss. They all had been temporary, yet ultimately inadequate, solutions to longing for Celeste.

But this night was a beast like a dragon in an old Albanian fairytale that he would love to mercilessly vanquish from his heart. The night was dark and empty; it enveloped him with sorrowful thoughts. It forced him to remember her; remember how terribly he'd missed her.

The coastal shores and the southern skies were beautiful. No doubt about it. They had always been an inseparable part of his past attempts to forget dark moments like these. But the vision of these picturesque vistas would not quell his pain this time. Francis was no longer consoled by their beauty. He did not care to try anymore. What was the point? His system had become resistant to their medicinal value. They could no longer make him happy.

How could Francis hope to ever really be happy if she were not in his arms? How could he pretend, or even aspire to be happy, if the sole reason for his life's happiness had vanished? Celeste was all he ever wanted, and now that she was gone, all joy had slowly been washed away from his life into the cracks of time.

Francis had even tried to make peace with God at times so that his divine power might create some sort of a miracle. But how could he make peace with the Divine with no peace in his heart first? How could he pretend to be at peace, if all the memories brought warring unrest to his mind, heart, and soul?

There were times when those memories began to drive Francis to the edge of dark despair. He had sometimes flirted with the somber and devilishly dreadful thought of trying to end his life by his own hand. He often believed it to be a more peaceful solution than endlessly longing for his missing soulmate. But whenever Francis felt pressed against the prickly loneliness of some dark night, he managed to step back from the suicidal precipice.

Francis knew that his death would ensure that he never see her again and snuff out the small flickering hope of their reunion. He would rather live in heartsick pain with the small promise of seeing her one day. To commit suicide would erase an improbable life journey that might lead him back to Celeste once again.

At the apex of all these thoughts, Francis looked on the top of his old desk. A pencil and paper. Through the years he had tried to reconstruct the past through a habit of writing short notes to himself to keep Celeste's memory alive. Francis had written many varied notes, touching upon subjects of all sorts. Some notes had been awash in bitterness and contempt. Especially, in a country where the idea of human rights was nothing but a false facade for the benefit of appeasing the proletariat. Most notes, however, were an outpouring of longing for his unrequited lover.

There was one note Francis had written not too long ago. He remembered it more vividly than any of the others because it was written to the Ionian Sea itself. He was inspired to write it while peacefully sitting on the Ionian shore of the coastal Albanian city.

Long ago, you carried with you my most precious love. You rescued her out of harm's way and brought her to safety. For that, I am eternally grateful to you. Not only am I grateful for that, but also at a loss for words to describe the magnitude of my appreciation for the things that you have meant to me.

Admiring your beauty and all your lovely attributes have become my lifelong occupation. You are a queen above all queens. Within your womb, you carry the most indispensable treasures of the world. You protect the secret from which life arises. You serve as the bridge between worlds, and I sometimes wish I could float on the undefined surface of your heavenly essence. I wish we could become one and create a divinely unique bond that can hold us together for eternity. I wish this because I know in my heart, living in the great beyond would be so much better with you.

But other than all these reasons, you are that much more special to me because when I look at you - I see her hazel eyes floating on crystallized tears. I see her breathtaking beauty gliding slowly onto the shifting shadows of the blue surface of the sea. I see one who always gave and never asked for anything in return.

Long ago, I may have lost her and maybe fate will make it so that I will never see her again. But whenever I miss her and need to see her - as I often do - I will turn to you and your infatuating natural beauty and glamour. For it is that perpetually regal beauty that will keep me going until the Gods intervene and say otherwise. I appreciate you for all the things that you have given; I admire you for the exquisite expressions of your flawless motions.

As I voice my appreciation, by thanking you endlessly for the hope that you bring to my shattered soul, I ask you one thing. Would you please carry with you in your soft coastal waves, guided through good times and bad, the certainty of my unwavering love for her every time I play the cello? Would you please carry with you, beneath the Sun or through the storms, my music so she could listen and dance to it one more time? Would you please?

Truly Yours,

Francis

This was perhaps the strongest note he had written during his time in southern Albania. He had titled it, "Beyond the Sea." Ironically, this short letter was not an outright confirmation of how he truly felt about the Ionian Sea. Francis did not always hold the sea itself with the kind of high regard described in the letter. At one point, years before writing it, he felt great disdain for the boundless body of water, simply because it reminded him of the day he and Celeste parted.

Suddenly, Francis grabbed the pencil, paused for a moment pregnant with inspiration and scribbled these lovingly familiar words:

Will you dance to my music?
Just so you won't forget me tomorrow.
Will you stay with me tomorrow?
So that I can tell you of my yesterdays . . .

Francis remembered this note more vividly than all the other short notes. He remembered it because he wrote these words all throughout the last twenty-eight years. The words resonated so deeply with him because they encapsulated how he pictured their life together. The note had become synonymous with his deep desire to spend eternity with her.

Thoughts of their last summer together swept through his mind like an irresistible wave. It was February 1941 when Francis' grandmother had become deathly ill. She understandably wanted to go back home and spend her last years in her native Albania. "Let's go visit your grandmother!" Celeste had suggested. So, the young couple decided to cross the vast Atlantic to see her in May.

They spent the entire time in Saranda, often going to picturesque local sites. The monastery of the Forty Saints, the ancient city of Butrint, and the island of Ksamil were all among some of the truly marvelous locations they visited during their brief stay.

The one site that instantly captivated them, however, was the Blue Eye. They discovered it accidentally while riding horses one late August evening. Instinctively, Celeste ran to the crystal-clear spring and let her hands glide across its briskly cold, turquoise surface. The coldness of the water sent chills throughout her body. Undeterred, she was momentarily taken aback, marveling at the beautiful descending Sun's reflection on the flowing water. She turned around to Francis instinctively and said: "make a wish!"

Francis gracefully approached her, lovingly held her face in his hands, gazed deep into her beautiful eyes under the setting Sun, "My wish is to be with you forever and ever my darling." Then he kissed Celeste softly on her lips, forehead, and cheeks while caressing each place he had kissed with his thumb.

Right there and then they gave in to their desires and made passionate love. They pressed against each other and felt the sensuous heat of their bodies merging. That night two lovers, who yearned eternally for one another, became one.

Two days later, Francis spontaneously urged her to leave Albania aboard a ship without him. The situation there was becoming dire. The Italian forces and Albanian rebels were fighting against each other across the country in full force. Francis knew it was no longer safe for Celeste to stay there, and it would be irresponsibly naive to assume the situation would soon improve.

Francis also tried to convince his ailing grandmother, but she refused to leave. She wanted nothing more than to spend her last years in the country that had gifted her with her first breath.

Celeste could not understand why they were unable to leave as a couple. "Let's go together," she cried and pleaded with him. All Francis could do was repeatedly reassure her that he would follow soon on a different ship and meet back in New York. They argued back and forth on the pier until Francis finally convinced her to leave without him. Celeste left Albania on the next available boat with tears pouring from her eyes.

After the war ended, Francis often thought of leaving Albania. But he'd always failed to do so. In fact, most times he had not dared to try. Almost no one was permitted to come in and out of the country. The few people that tried were captured and either killed on the spot or imprisoned for life. Francis had tried to pick the right time to escape, but that 'right time' never presented itself. Year after year, the Cold War tensions between East and West and the Albanian Communist Party's domestic restrictions on its citizens' free movement never eased enough for Francis to escape. Even now that almost three decades have passed, the chances are still nonexistent.

Now the possibility of escaping was so unlikely that Francis had begun treating it as a cruel joke.

"If you're so obsessed with your American culture then you should start thinking of a way to get out of here," Nikolla joked with him one day.

"I am too old now. If I had a younger physique, athletic strength, or energy, then I'd give it a thought. And then I'd take you with me."

"Get away from me with those damned temptations!" Nikolla loudly responded, gesturing with his hands as if dusting off the devil himself.

Both men laughed.

In most of their recent conversations, Nikolla had promised him that he'd help him leave Albania. There had been several instances when the sensitive subject had seriously come up between the two of them. However, it had been Nikolla, his old Kosovar friend, that had initiated the subject of escape. He had soberly insisted several times that Francis should return to his American home and dreams. The most recent occasion Nikolla revisited the subject was two nights ago, immediately after a discussion about American music.

"You may be fascinated with the natural beauty of Albania's southern shores. You may love its culture and people. But this is not for you, Francis. Maybe, under a different government, you could have lived here with a family, with Celeste. No doubt about it. But you are a freethinker, a lover of music and literature. Heck, you're even a poet by the way you always talk. It is such a shame that you have become a prisoner of your own ideas. You came here searching for a country and a culture, but it does not want you in return. You don't belong here. You belong in a free society. I know that you feel lost here and I promise that I will get you out soon," Nikolla said.

When Nikolla spoke those words, he superseded all his previous statements on the greatness and glory of the State and the Communist Party. Through these utterances, he was implying that there were large, inherent flaws in a government that suppressed the human character, its artistic creativity, their citizens' individual rights. Perhaps this Kosovar gentleman had realized these negative realities long ago but had somehow remained silently content with living a monotonic life in a country that he could call his own.

Francis listened to Nikolla's lecture two nights ago and realized that all his words had rung truth. But in all fairness, it was not the Albanian people or its culture that had never loved him back. It was the system, its' oppressively bureaucratic political juggernaut that had imprisoned human values and free intellect. The individual was nothing. The Party was above all.

It was useless now to contemplate what could have been or should have been. He considered his life now a fait accompli, a notion of the past. Now there was nothing he could do, nothing he could change. All that remained were his suppressed values, lost love, and distant memories.

After all these years, Francis wasn't sure if she was alive or dead. Celeste could have married someone over the years. Probably she was a doctor or a lawyer as her mother had wanted. Perhaps a successful ballerina. "She was an excellent dancer, no doubt about it," he always thought. And as much as he wanted to keep her memory alive, he always caught himself thinking about her in past tense, frozen as that gorgeous teenage girl with whom he had fallen so deeply in love.

Each time Francis caught himself thinking of her and their past together, music played through his mind and relaxed him. He would allow the music to become his escape to their magical moments, a route to those points in time when life seemed so simple. He would devour those memories and drown in their lost love.

This was exactly what this night had become. It transported him to memories that made his distant past seem so close and so real. Francis let his old record player play the kind of music that brought her back to him, even if only fondly in his memory. Music was his emotional outlet, his ship to loving shores, his best friend like baseball or cello had been back in the States.

Francis was now in the mood again to listen to more music from the 1930s era. Slowly he got up from his bed and walked to the little stand where the record player rested. He removed the old record from the turntable and replaced it with another.

Then he walked back to his bed. He tossed and turned in bed desperately wishing the mattress were a little more comfortable. Francis made a mental note to get more cotton to stuff in the mattress the next time he went into town.

At that moment, he was about to let himself float musically through his fond memories. Yet again. But the journey was short-lived. There were suddenly knocks on the door. Francis begrudgingly lifted himself from the old, uncomfortable mattress, irritated that someone had disturbed his languid comfort. Who could it be at twelve o 'clock at night; an imaginary beast; a ghostly specter of the night? If that were the case, who could have woken them up? Francis walked through the narrow corridor, now worried because he never had visitors at this time.

KNOCK! KNOCK! The sound grew louder and more urgent as he approached the front door.

"I'm coming, I am coming!" Francis responded to the knocks.

He lifted the latch and pulled the door open. Instantly, he became dumbfounded by who he was seeing. He looked at the person standing before him as consonants and vowels became instantly frozen on his tongue. He tried to forcibly form a word but his lips simply could not utter a sound of it.

Two Visitors

"Nina…" he finally whispered under his breath.

"Hello Francis!" she smilingly greeted him with clear and gentle voice. "May I come in?"

At first, his mind did not comprehend her words. Struck by her sudden appearance, he stood listlessly frozen and unresponsive in the doorway. Francis had not seen Nina in over five years and now here she stood, beautiful as the first day he' d ever seen her. Standing behind her gracious and serene visage, stood an unidentifiable ghost-like shadowy shape Francis did not initially recognize.

"Yes! Please come in!" Francis responded after a brief hesitation.

As Nina moved forward, the unknown figure emerged from the darkness into the ambient light of the porch lantern. Francis nearly collapsed from shock. It was the sinister looking man dressed in black from his confrontation in the principal's office.

The three walked into the living room.

"To what do I owe this visit?" Francis asked, confused by the sudden visit's intentions and urgently trying to conceal his nervous apprehension.

"Francis, I would like to introduce you to Arben. He is an old friend of mine. I believe you two met earlier today."

Francis had heard his name before but had never known what he looked like. Nina had mentioned 'Arben' to him years ago as an ex-boyfriend who had walked out of her life several years prior to her meeting Francis.

Francis remained transfixed by this surprise visit so late at night, especially knowing Arben had recently been at the principal's office. Most important, however, was that Arben worked for the Albanian Secret Police.

"There is something important that we have to discuss," Arben said in a disturbingly calm manner. "What I am about to tell you has to remain between us in this room. No one else can know. Do you understand?"

Francis nodded his head in silent agreement, though he remained unsure if this conversation would warrant his silence.

"I understand you come from a different world from ours, though not many people here are aware of that. Honestly, I was unaware of it either until recently when Nina and her family mentioned you."

"What exactly are you referring to?" Francis asked with a direct tone.

"Before I get to that, I would like to inform you that after our little encounter earlier today, the principal came to my hotel room and asked that I investigate you. He told me that there are certain elements in your character that he finds troublesome. He said he suspects that you are up to something. For the good of the State, he told me he is ready to denounce you."

"Denounce me? Denounce me for what? What am I suspected of being 'up to'?" Francis fidgeted slightly on the old couch, growing increasingly irritated by the sound of the vague and baseless accusations.

"I don't know. You tell me!" Arben watched Francis' eyes sternly with an impishly ironic smile.

"I hope you're not implying that you believe him," Francis replied, getting up slightly from the couch to signal his protestation.

"I came here to inform you as a courtesy. Obviously, I am not here formerly accusing you. I am also not saying that I don't believe him," Arben took out a cigarette case as if in the park for a Sunday stroll and not in Francis' living room after midnight hinting at treason.

"I know what you are thinking. Why am I here in your home after midnight?" Arben's mouth smiled warmly while lighting up a cigarette, yet his eyes remained fixed and piercing like a hawk to its prey. "I just want to find the underlying cause of this. I too, am not clear on the principal's intent. He does not have any factual evidence, yet he is eagerly willing to press ahead with his denunciation of you. I asked him to think thoroughly before he decided to proceed because of the dire consequences of his accusations. But he's convinced that you're a reactionary imperialist and that you have, on several occasions, demonstrated a character with counter-revolutionary Western tendencies."

"And so, he came and told you all this?"

"It is much worse than that I'm afraid. He has scheduled a meeting with the Party's First Secretary tomorrow morning to make these accusations."

"I don't understand. How can someone make such an argument without factual evidence?"

"They don't need a reason. All they need to do is carry out a search of your house and find music they deem to be unsuitable," Nina interrupted pleadingly.

"By 'they' you mean 'him'?" Francis angrily asked, motioning his head directly to Arben.

"Francis, if I wanted to raid your house, I would have done so tomorrow afternoon after the principal forces the issue in front of the entire town council."

"Well, I am ready to defend myself. I've done nothing wrong, and I will simply explain to the council that I am being set up falsely."

"Are you willing to take that risk? Do you realize that once he denounces you, it could potentially lead to imprisonment or deportation to Burrel Prison labor camp?"

"I have no other choice. It's not as if I can run away from this unjustifiable threat."

"Franc, you do have a choice and we can help you," Nina said calmly.

"Before we get into that, there are some other things that I want to discuss," Arben quickly intervened. "Let me start by saying that Nina and her family have nothing but wonderful things to say about you. Though I may not know her family, I do trust Nina emphatically."

Nina humbly lowered her gaze at Arben's praise.

"Apart from the principal's vague accusations," Arben continued, "I don't understand why he hadn't mentioned your supposedly treasonous behavior before you came to his office. Then, hours later, was so feverishly willing to turn you in."

"You should ask him these questions yourself. I don't have to explain myself when I don't even know my crime."

"Francis, I am not here only as a friend of a friend, but also as a great fan of your music. I am trying to help you as much as I can. But I am also trying to do my due diligence in my official capacity. Ultimately, I want to be assured that, at the end of the day, I can still live with my decision." Arben spoke sincerely.

"Well, I'm trying to live with myself too," Francis retorted. "And I know that I haven't done anything wrong. I've always tried to do the right thing here. I will try and present my side, though I understand that manipulatively conniving people of the world like the principal, will probably win."

"What is it that you did that you think was right?" Arben asked keenly.

"I defended a little child because I believed my unscrupulous accuser had disciplined him too harshly for not following the dress code."

Arben looked at him curiously.

"My friend's son, one of my students, had not followed the dress code to the exact letter," Francis continued.

"Yeah, I heard about it. It was Nina's nephew. The principal sent him home."

"No. More like… he first punished him harshly and then sent him away," Francis replied. "Listen. I have no problem with the principal's admonition of the student if it's for the overall benefit of the community. But the boy simply forgot his scarf. How does that fall into such category?"

"Is this what this is all about?" Arben asked, continuing his line of questioning.

Francis nodded. "God forbid anyone ever slightly questions this man's authority!"

Now Arben stood up from the couch, shoved his hands in his pants' pockets, and began to nervously circle the room. He did not mutter a single word. Instead, he continued silently pacing. It was obvious that whatever was on his mind was of extremely significant importance.

"You are a good man Francis," said Arben finally standing still. "It is a shame that you did what was right and somehow will still get punished for it. The principal, it seems, is an extremely dangerous man. He will not rest until he gets what he wants, you behind bars or worse. I know it and you know it! However, what the principal does not know is what I discovered today. And when he finds out, he will certainly want to use it to denounce you in the absence of any other evidence. And believe me, he will!"

"What are you talking about?" Francis asked, perplexed by the sudden confusing turn of the conversation.

"You're a foreigner, Francis. You were not born here, and it is only a matter of time before the principal finds that out," said Arben, methodically lighting yet another cigarette.

"But it's not as if I've kept this hidden from anyone. Everyone knows that I am not a native Albanian. What does that have to do with anything?" Francis confessed.

"It has to do with everything! I know how people like this principal operate. I have dealt with his type for a while now, and one thing is certain. Once he finds out that you were born in the West, he will say that you are some sort of Western spy. He will no longer be satisfied with simply accusing you of being a counter-revolution reactionary, but a spy of the imperialist powers bent on Albanian destruction! He will make it all up to ensure his case sticks. Then, you will become the subject of a giant investigation and your whole life put under a microscope from which you will never escape. And once news of your upbringing travels to the capital, his accusations will be nearly impossible for the Party to ignore. You will be physically abused and tortured while in prison, especially once they remember that you refused to remain a musician in the capital years ago. How you stubbornly said no to a government in need of you to represent them and help them gain positive international notoriety. No longer will you be remembered as one of the best musicians this nation ever witnessed, but as one of nation's most notorious villains sent to sow internal discord. Is that how you want to be remembered, Francis Petrela?"

Francis thought this over. All he had contributed artistically or intellectually to the people of Albania would have meant nothing, have resulted in nothing, and have produced nothing. In its place would instead be lies and deception used as a fiendish plot to justify his eventual character assassination.

"That is not how I want my life to be remembered," Francis fervently said while remaining seated. He was still in shock by the dire implications of this potential scenario. "Ok, what do you propose?"

"I propose…" Arben paused for a moment and looked at Nina this time, "we propose that you pack quickly and lightly and go!"

"Go? Go where? I have nowhere to go!"

"Francis, you have to go back where you came from. It is the only solution," Arben implored. "If you stay here, the principal will press on with his accusations. However, if you disappear, he will have no ability to go further with his case. Even if he chooses to pursue the case, he will have to accuse a phantom and ask the State to chase a ghost."

Francis was so confused, he wondered if his mind was playing tricks on him. "Am I dreaming?" He wanted to pinch himself. Maybe he had fallen asleep to the music on his uncomfortable bed, he thought.

"Francis, please believe me. You have got to go, right now. We have already prepared everything. Pack your most indispensable belongings and come with us," Nina said with a calm, but firm voice.

Francis stopped asking questions and went into his room. Nina followed behind to help him pack some essentials. Then he hid some records inside folded clothes. As he was about to place the old gramophone in another piece of luggage, he noticed Nina scoldingly staring at him.

"Well, I don't even know where I am going. And I am not leaving this behind," Francis said nervously.

Nina placed her hand lovingly on his cheek to calm him. "There is no reason to be nervous. I never meant you harm, and you know that. Trust me."

"I am not leaving this behind," Francis argued, his voice still trembling.

"Alright, but nothing else."

"Not even the cello," he asked with eyes begging.

Nina looked in his eyes with pitiful awe. She wanted to break down and cry, suddenly realizing how unfulfilled his life had been. "Broken soul, shattered dreams," she thought as her eyes welled up with tears.

"You will always remain our Albanian Mozart!"

When they finally finished packing, Francis turned momentarily and looked at the cello, abandoned and alone in a corner of the room. He flipped off the light switch. The room now dark and still.

The three of them headed out onto the gravel path toward the wooden fence. The gravel crunched beneath their feet. For a moment, Francis looked back at the old, now abandoned house. The only light now was the small flickering flame of the lantern. "This decision is essential for my spiritual survival," Francis thought. They carefully made their way onto the dark driveway and inside an old Skoda and drove away.

***

Here, it is worth noting that Arben was the young man who walked out of Nina's life years before. He'd seemingly fallen off the face of the earth and taken with him a part of Nina's heart. Unbeknownst to her, during these missing years, he worked as a secret police agent with the Albanian National Security. As such, his primary responsibility was to ensure the safety of Albanian national interests.

Arben had proudly served his purpose, though at times he had to close his eyes to the ways of some of his colleagues. They frequently fabricated some of the nation's most notorious so-called 'threats' simply to justify the trial of some innocent and respectable people. However, his greatest fulfillment in life was his ability to live with a clean conscience. He was confident that he had always performed his duties honestly, thoroughly and diligently.

In his line of work, Arben had met people in high and low places in society. That is how he had initially learned of Francis' music. "You should go and see this guy play," said one of the powerful Party bosses. And the musician had not disappointed. Francis' finest musical performance, as Arben would recall later in life, had helped the security agent understand the power of music and appreciate its deeper emotional meaning. He had realized that music was like a sponge that soaked up and cleaned away the filth that he came across in his line of work. The lies and all the negativity washed away and instead replaced with purpose, meaning, and something of beauty that made life worth living.

Arben had been a security agent for a long time and had enough experience to understand that Francis was not a real threat to national security. Somehow, he wanted to save Francis from becoming a victim of someone else's intrigues and petty personal vendettas.

He had thought long and hard about it after the principal had left the hotel room earlier that late afternoon. Arben spent countless hours brainstorming multiple contingencies to help Francis. In the end, the location for the most sensible plan to get Francis out of the country would be on the outskirts of Konispol, a small village nearby the Albanian-Greek border.

In the surrounding outskirts of the village, a man waited for them in the dark. A contact Arben trusted with his life. This man worked as the head of the Albanian Guard, in charge of patrolling the Albanian-Greek border. He had agreed to lead Francis along a safe passage across the border and away from the border guard.

***

When Francis found out about this hastily hatched plan, he was astounded. He never saw any of this coming. He did not know whether the plan was real or some sort of elaborate scheme to entrap him. The Albanian Communist Party had become infamous through their years in power for setting people up with perjured testimony at bogus trials, baseless accusations, and mass humiliation of political dissidents. In most cases, the victims were dragged out of their homes along dark secluded roads where they were either tortured or simply assassinated. Francis did not know whether tonight he would fall into one of these tragic scenarios.

In an instant, his mind went back to Nikolla. Why had he not come with Arben to see him off and wish him well? Where was he? This was out of character for the gentleman from Kosovo. Perhaps, Francis worried, the Secret Police agents had arrested and tortured him to force him to talk. "Maybe, they got to him," he thought.

"By the way, Nikolla is waiting for us in Konispol," Nina calmly answered as if reading Francis' growing concerns.

However, Francis still did not know whether or not to completely believe her. But again, he was torn. This was Nina, the southern beauty who had fallen deeply in love with her so-called Albanian Mozart fifteen years ago. There would be no way that she could mean for any harm to come to him, he thought.

Francis was more concerned with Arben's intentions and motives. After such a prolonged period of absence, this man had suspiciously returned to Nina's life, claiming to want to help the foreign-born ex-boyfriend of his former lover. An ex-boyfriend whose purported American values directly contravened the principles and policies of his beloved Communist Manifesto. Arben's involvement with helping Francis escape if discovered, could end both his career and his life.

So, where did all this eagerness to help Francis come from? And why would Arben help Francis escape?

Right now, none of this made any sense to him.

There was another detail that had started to bother Francis. He couldn't exactly pin down the details though or remember it clearly. He tried to recall their conversation, the trivial things he may have ignored during his panic-induced rush of adrenaline. Perhaps, something insignificant; perhaps, something crucially important.

Perhaps something that was unsaid happened in the room while Nina was helping him pack. He closed his eyes tightly in concentration to try and remember. Nope, nothing he could think of seemed out of the ordinary. Only the memory of Nina's tear-filled eyes as she confessed that Francis would always remain an Albanian Mozart.

Maybe, there was some behavior out of the ordinary with Arben that went unnoticed. What exactly had he been doing in the living room while they packed the suitcases? Come to think of it, Arben might have secretly had a walkie-talkie with him or maybe a hidden recording device taping their conversation somehow. Nope. Francis couldn't remember seeing or hearing anything like that, not even as they walked through the wooden gates.

Francis thought to himself, "What is it? Come on think, don't lose your composure now. There must have been a tiny detail that was said. There was a word. What was the word that triggered all of this?"

Konispol…

Right, Konispol. That was it! That was the missing piece of the puzzle. He knew that place. It was a small agricultural town in the Saranda district. Though Francis had never been there during all his thirty years in Albania, somehow its name had come up before in a conversation. Which conversation though?

Francis vaguely remembered there was someone once that mentioned something about the town. There was a man… perhaps twenty years ago… an older man. He was a local.

A local man mentioned something about some other locals…

The locals…

That was yet another piece of this frustrating puzzle. Suddenly, he felt his muscle tense up as if demons had quickly gotten a deathly tight grip on his aging physique.

Years ago, Francis had heard that some of the locals discovered a dead body in the woods, viciously massacred by a machine gun. They believed it was the body of someone who had tried to cross the border to Greece. Everyone suspected the body had been purposely left there to be discovered. It was a warning sign to the town of the deadly consequences for anyone who got caught trying to flee the country.

Suddenly, these dark fearful thoughts filled Francis' mind and had him feverishly wanting to jump out of the moving truck.

"What if this was all an elaborate scheme to remove him from the country without a struggle? What if there was a machine gun hidden somewhere in this truck to be later used for his execution?"

Despite all his fears, Francis decided not to act on his paranoia by opening the truck door. He instead focused his mind on remembering a vague image of beautiful Celeste's face and how much he longed to hold her again in his arms. He had spent almost his entire adult life trying to keep a picture of her every detail in his mind. Sadly, over the years his memory of her face had slowly faded.

Perhaps, this was not a sham. Maybe, this was his last opportunity to leave what had become his utopian trap away from the world and chase something tangible. Tangible enough to pursue his loves and dreams in the country where he had taken his first breath. At that moment, while speeding down this bumpy country road in the dead of night, Francis became willing to risk it all. To reach out for what he should have snatched a long time ago. His American way of life and his love for the United States. It was time to renew himself. Time to reclaim the missing pieces of his gloriously happy past.

The Escape

When they finally reached the outskirts of Konispol, Nikolla was already waiting there for them. "This is a new life for you Francis," Nikolla said with a stuttering voice choking back his tears. "I told you, I'd get you out." Speechless with gratitude, Francis looked admirably at the gentleman from Kosovo. He had finally shed his tough demeanor and tried to smile despite the tears in his eyes.

After the two men hugged, Francis turned to Nina, the Albanian beauty who had briefly entered his heart years ago. Her big emerald eyes were welled up with tears. He walked towards her, and gently extended his arm to wipe a teardrop from the corner of her eye. She tried to move her lips but was too overcome with emotions to make a sound. He could make out what she was trying to say by reading her quivering lips: "You'll always remain our Albanian Mozart."

As he was about to walk away, he looked at Arben with such a tremendous amount of gratitude and appreciation. "Thank you!" Francis firmly extended his hand. Mixed with his gratitude, however, were also feelings of guilt for doubting Arben's motives only moments before. Arben met his gaze and nodded in acceptance as he extended his hand to complete the men's earnest handshake. "I meant it when I said you are the best musician I have ever heard." Francis smiled in humble gratitude for Arben's kind words.

"My friend here will walk with you up to a certain point to ensure your safety," Arben spoke one last time.

Francis bent slightly to pick up the suitcases and turned around once again to look at Nikolla, the man with whom he'd shared countless of conversations on every topic. They smiled warmly at each other.

This moment, they both knew, would be the last time they would see each other.

Francis and the man that Arben had placed in charge of his safety walked silently in the dark for more than twenty minutes. They walked with great caution because the roads and the pathways were bumpy and poorly paved. Once they finally reached the part of the forest where the trees were the densest, his unnamed chaperone said flatly, "Past this point, you're on your own. Cut right through the forest and you'll end up in Greece."

Francis thanked him and, once the man was out of sight, looked around to get his bearings. Everything was still and dark, with only the cascading moonlight lighting his way. Should he fear the unknown that awaited him within this dense forest? Or embrace the unknown that lies ahead to achieve his freedom? For some peculiar reason, the way he imagined these two choices, these two paths flipped a sort of decisive switch in his mind. He could no longer vacillate about his choices or speculate about their potential outcomes. He simply wanted to get all this fear and uncertainty over with. So, he ran.

On that dark night, Francis felt a profound sense of loss and loneliness slapping him in the face. Those years had come and gone and now he was alone, running in a pitch-black forest, carrying all his worldly possessions. He was running for his right to live, to dream, and to be free. He was running for the joy of reuniting with people from his past, to love and hold them again. He was running back to the life that he had once abandoned.

While he ran, Francis would periodically look behind him, but each time was relieved to find there was no sign of pursuit. The more he feverishly ran along the secluded path, far away from the main road, the more he was struck by the utter stillness of the forest. The night's enveloping darkness was now absolute, and the weight of its silence reigned over everything like a queen's terror on her subjects. As he frantically ran for his life, everything around him was frozen in solitude.

As Francis ran into the enveloping solitude, further away from the last point of human contact, another aspect of the forest started to unveil itself to him. The night's stillness was no longer absolute, new elements began to emerge.

There were the eerie sounds of cold spiraling winds whistling through the steep hills along the border area. These whistles pierced the silence like a sharpened knife. The same knife that would be used by the Secret Police to torture him if he were caught. This mental image made the necessity of his escape that much more urgent. However, the approaching challenge of having to cross these steep hills, lying between him and the border, remained a daunting task. Looking at the hills, Francis felt a rising sense of impending defeat, as if some higher powers were intent on stopping him from this daring attempt. The blinding darkness, the biting cold, the rugged terrain, and the inevitable exposure of sunrise. These imminent dangers would be unforgiving throughout his escape and were undeterrable acts of Mother Nature's fury unleashed upon Francis in the depths of the forest.

For some strange reason, these approaching hills reminded him of the Alps in northern Albania. Francis had been there once during the war, and though they were hundreds of miles away, he couldn't help but see the resemblance on a smaller scale. In the Alps, he'd seen a great deal of snow while climbing over the steep mountains to push back the Germans Army's advance. Back then the snows had presented the greatest challenge for him.

But in southern Albania, and especially during this time of the year, there was no sign of snow. Even more, these hills were nowhere near as high as the mountain range of the Alps. But under extremely strenuous and stressful circumstances such as these, the mind often seeks small irrational parallels and illogical patterns to make life's obstacles seem insurmountable. It is only in human nature.

Francis looked at the sky. The sky was an unbroken sea of grey as though an ominously foreboding sign from some angry ancient God.

Perhaps, a hailstorm is coming, he thought while the freezing wind was bellowing. Its cold cutting right through his cheeks and ears. How was this all possible in the early Autumn? Or was this once again his mind superseding reality by creating these imaginary conditions?

As the first drops of rain started to fall, Francis came across a narrow stream. Without any hesitation, he stepped over it to avoid getting wet. The path was becoming nearly impossible to see because of the increasingly thick fog surrounding him. Several times he stumbled, dropping his small suitcase as he fell, and injuring his knees and elbows. Once, a fall ended up with his face splattered in a big pile of mud. However, Francis remained undeterred by any of these problems and kept walking to his freedom and away from certain persecution.

He was on a journey. One whose destination was almost four thousand miles away. He was on a mission now to reach that destination, running through whatever pain and obstacles he must endure. A mission, he now realized, that should have been completed three decades ago. Francis ran on for another 15 to 20 minutes when something grabbed his attention. Amongst the stillness of the forest, he heard a faint sound nearby. It sounded to Francis like footsteps walking across fallen branches. He immediately stopped, frozen in place, and looked toward the general direction of the sound. He could see nothing irregular there.

As he was about to run, he heard the sounds again. But this time it sounded as though it was getting closer and closer. Francis looked around trying frantically to determine the direction of the movement. At first, he couldn't tell, but as it became more distinctive, he spotted some shadows moving in the fog. Suddenly, he felt like a deer caught in headlights. He felt panic, lost as to where to go or what to do.

The shadows slowly moved closer and closer as Francis remained rooted to the spot, frozen in time, in immovable agony for the years he had lost. He felt trapped, perhaps by figments of his own paranoid perceptions, or perhaps by the reality of the attempted escape. Suddenly, he dropped the small suitcases and in this moment of weakness tried summoning all his inner strength. He knelt and closed his eyes.

"My Lord forgive me if I've ever done you wrong!"

For the first time since the war, he made the sign of the cross across his chest.

Letters of The Past

Early Fall, 1970. Francis watched the Sun's rays sprinkled through the heavy humid air. The scattered clouds moved slowly across the azure sky and made way for a new day's brilliant noon. Out on the distant horizon, the sunlight casts a godlike halo. The rain had stopped at last.

After enjoying the magnificent view, Francis knelt on his left knee and went straight to work. With a small sickle in his hands, he cut the ridiculously overgrown grass that obviously had not been tended to in a few years. Occasionally, he checked for weeds and would vigorously pull them out when discovered.

Half an hour passed and now the September Sun was steaming hot. Francis repeatedly wiped his forehead with his sleeve in a battle against the sweat drops which were continuously covering his face. The thick humid air and the height of the fierce Sun made quite a fiery duo. He stood up and walked to the steps, where he happily grabbed a plastic water bottle.

After gulping down the water, he grabbed a baseball on the ground nearby and tossed it against the wall. With each throw, he bounced it increasingly harder. His anger growing for all the years he had not been able to do this simple act.

After repeating the routine for about ten minutes, Francis walked into the house, down the long hallway, and into the kitchen. Francis stood in the kitchen looking out at the blazing Sun and drank a cold bottle of Amstel beer. Then, he took a cool shower to wash off the early Autumn sweat.

Feeling refreshed and clean, Francis walked into the living room. There, sitting crookedly on the couch, sat an old, wrinkle-faced lady with gloomy eyebrows. She was a solitary figure whose every movement conveyed the weight of all the years she had endured.

He slowly walked toward the couch and knelt beside her. Francis kissed her witheringly frail hands and held them against his chest. She reciprocated his love by kissing his forehead repeatedly with tears streaming from her eyes. She kissed the son, thought lost forever, with a mother's tears of joy.

For twenty-nine years, she heard people say he had been killed in the war. Some said he was imprisoned or that he defected and became an agent. A few guessed he'd been detained by the government in Albania against his will. Nonetheless, she had patiently waited for him by the window, day after day. And when those days turned to nights, she'd sleep near the window while hopefully dreaming for her son's return.

When Francis had returned home, nearly four weeks ago, Anna was completely shocked. She saw a strange man at her doorstep, not realizing that he was her son. Now twenty-nine years older and grayer and eerily resembling her late husband. They both stood motionless in the doorway for a moment. Both speechlessly transfixed with the sight of the other after so many years. Anna began to recognize those chestnut brown eyes and the characteristic brow. She found herself helplessly trembling and weak in the knees as her mind began processing the image for which her heart had yearned for so long. She had been living alone for the past four years since Francis' father died. Now she found a reason to live again.

For Francis, Anna was his entire world now. His only living parent, she had been the person who first instilled and nurtured his love of music. Once, she had been young, beautiful and vibrant. But the years of worry about her son's fate and the recent loss of her beloved husband had taken its toll on her. Now she was a frail elderly lady in the twilight of life.

His father Luke also had become quite weak in the years before his death in 1965. Francis' disappearance in 1941 had left him emotionally wandering during the intervening 24 years, through feelings of hopelessness, depression, and guilt. Painful years of accumulated emotional suffering had physically taken its toll on him. Eventually, Luke's heart gave out with his son's name on his lips on his deathbed.

Francis could not believe how much things had changed. How much he'd missed. He wanted to burst into tears and let all his emotions flow uncontrollably. He wanted to grief the loss of a father, the man who had taken him to his first Yankees game. He wanted to mourn the passing of a parent who taught him everything about the simple things in life. He wanted to unleash all the years of his sorrow. But he knew he had to remain strong for his now fragile mother like his father had been until his last breath.

Francis walked into his old study room and sat at the piano. His mother had thankfully preserved it and dusted it every day, always convinced that one day her son would return and play it. Over the last four weeks since his return, Francis had happily played, despite the rust in his once graceful fingers. He played the old Irving Berlin song 'Cheek to Cheek' but something about it felt wrong. Maybe it was because his life was so far from the heaven mentioned in the lyrics and so his lonely heart could not sing the way it once had.

During all his years in Albania, Francis had hoped to one day return to the American dream. But now that he was back, his once perfect world was still far from being restored. The United States engaged in an ugly, increasingly unpopular, war in Vietnam. American soldiers were dying left and right as Communism across the globe seemed to be prevailing. The American economy was hurting as ideological, generational, and racial differences in its society were widening into intractable divisions.

In addition, Francis was continuing to have the same terrible dreams he had been having in southern Albania. Dreams that would always leave him out of breath and feeling hopelessness. Life without

Celeste, his father, and so many people from the past left him with the same tormented feelings from Saranda.

***

His closest remaining friend in New York was Jonathan. He would show up every night at Francis' house, usually around nine o'clock at night, and tell Francis about his experiences fighting in the Second World War. Jonathan wistfully recounted how it had all started for him in the winter of 1941 when the Japanese attacked Pearl Harbor. His younger sister Kansas, who had been a nurse at the Hawaiian naval base, was one of the many people killed during that fateful day.

Without his sister and best friend, Johnny was one of the first volunteers in his neighborhood to enlist in the military. He joined General Patton's famed Seventh Army, with revenge in his heart. After a brief stint in North Africa, he went on to help capture Sicily. He had seen it all. Murderous mortar shells flying over his head and splitting the earth under his feet. Close friends dropping like flies with their souls deceived by naïve notions of patriotism, and their young bodies shattered by artillery. Johnathan said he had been up to his neck in death. Remembering the horrors of these experiences and the current American bloodshed in Southeast Asia, he and Francis agreed that there was never any glory in war, and never would be. For war stripped anyone who experiences it of their innocence and dreams.

Sometimes, while in Sicily, Johnny looked out across the Adriatic Sea, wondering whether Francis still lived in Albania. He even flirted with the idea of taking a daring trip across the sea to reunite with his best friend. But he couldn't bring himself to leave a band of brothers behind enemy lines.

After returning home, Johnathan married Julia, one of Francis' first cousins. They had two sons, who he endlessly and unashamedly spoiled. Occasionally, he would play catch with them when his work schedule permitted. He worked full-time as a crew chief umpire for the Major League Baseball Association. Obviously, the love for the game had never left him. He playfully assured Francis that he still would call strikes on players anytime they got rowdy or kicked dirt on his precious home plate.

Francis was amazed at how much Jonathan had changed over the years. In Francis' mind, the people and places of his childhood had been frozen for the last three decades. However, the flow of time leaves nothing unchanged. Jonathan, the once playful and slightly jerky kid, had matured into a respectable, reliable and responsible adult. He was a great husband to his wife and a model father to their two sons. "Age functions the same for everybody," Francis thought to himself.

Jonathan was glad that Francis had finally returned home. To him, Francis had been a best friend, a younger brother, and a confidante. Now, whenever possible, he would visit, and they would discuss baseball and the years Francis had missed in America. Among those things, was how the 'Iron Horse' had finally lost his battle with the dreadful, newly named Lou Gehrig's disease on June 2, 1941, weeks after Francis and Celeste had left for Albania. Francis stood silently still upon Jonathan recounting the death of an American icon. It was another moment when he knew the chance of renewing his old life was forever shattered.

The subject of Celeste had come up once several weeks before. According to Johnny, Celeste had come asking for any news of him for seven years after returning from Albania. She would cry buckets of tears during each visit. Eventually, she stopped visiting all together and no one knew her whereabouts. "Later on, I read her name on some article once," Johnny concluded. "I think she became a big shot ballerina."

Francis wondered about her repeated visits during that seven-year period. In the Bible, the number seven always symbolized completion. For six days, God created the world with perfection and on the seventh, he rested from his labors. Did her seven years have any significance to it? "What a useless analysis," he thought. It was simply love, and her unconditional devotion that made her come back.

Since his return to the States, Francis had not made any real attempts to locate her. Only once, a couple weeks ago, he had taken a cab to her old house. His eyes were blurry as he had approached it. His stomach tight. A feeling of relentless anticipation. However, he had found a different family there. No sign of her. Heartbroken, beaten and consumed with her memory of three decades, he needed to come to terms with his past now. This final chapter of momentary hopes and doubts had finally ended. "Besides, if she became as successful as Johnny led me to believe," Francis thought "she surely moved on with her life." He would have to remember her forever as his unrequited love.

He stretched his arms above his head and loudly cracked his knuckles. Francis let his hands briefly hover over the piano keys and then started playing the undulating sixteenth notes from Camille Saint-Saens' "The Dying Swan." This part of the musical piece is supposed to evoke the graceful movement of a swan's feet beneath the water.

***

Two weeks after returning to New York City, Francis took a cab ride to an old familiar place on Broadway, Astoria. He was pleasantly surprised to see Café Place still there after all these years. "It is the atmosphere in the café itself that makes us keep going back time and time again," he fondly remembered Celeste writing decades ago in a school essay.

The place still possessed that same romantic atmosphere he remembered. The sunlight streamed through its copious windows and young couples held hands as they gazed longingly at each other. He immediately realized he was the oldest one there and began to feel a little uncomfortable and out of place. However, his self-consciousness was interrupted when he looked at the wall near the entrance. He was pleasantly surprised to see a bulletin board there with several little notes pinned to it. "Love notes," he thought with a smile in his heart.

"It's really gratifying to see this place still here after all these years," he said to the young waitress. "Thanks, but it didn't look very promising during our grand opening night," the waitress smiled back, "but it's really picked up a lot in the last eighteen months."

Francis was confused by her choice of words. The Café Place had opened its doors over thirty years ago, long before her time there.

"What do you mean by grand opening?"

"The place was shut down for two years before a new owner bought it three summers ago," she answered politely.

Now her earlier answer made sense, so he did not ask for more information. Instead, he shifted attention to the bulletin board.

"What is that all about," he asked, his eyes glued to the board.

"Oh, it is something nice we do for our customers. Whoever wants can share any sort of statement or poem they desire by writing on that bulletin board."

"Love is timeless," he said to her.

After the waitress left, he scribbled some thoughtful words of his own.

While remembering this episode, Francis continued to play the undulating sixteenth notes on the piano. He visualized Celeste on their first night together at the Bohemian Hall as she gracefully danced "The Dying Swan." Now he wondered whether Celeste was still the tall, slender, beautiful ballerina that she once was.

***

Earlier in that same day and one borough away, she sat alone at a table in her favorite coffee shop. She rested her head on her folded arms, looking from afar as if a lifetime of defiance had finally worn her out. The store had been slightly flooded when she arrived in the morning; the rain had fallen hard overnight. She had helped the staff clean up the water. Mops had gotten soaked, buckets had been filled, and brooms had been sweeping the remainder of the refuse. As usual, she never shied away from challenging work or getting her hands dirty. She was always committed to lead her staff by example.

Now she stopped to rest awhile in the coffee shop. She held a small piece of paper in her hands. She wondered if she had ever put it down during the last two weeks. She struggled with the written contents and desperately tried to make sense of this small note.

Searching for you has become my lifelong struggle and I've written millions of words that no one understands. But I do not mind repeatedly explaining it to them because not even thousands of piles of elaborately written romantic letters can describe the love that I hold for you. My love flies effortlessly somewhere out in the Orion constellation at dusk and then returns to Earth at dawn every day. Only a fool like me can be brave enough to admit my eternal love for you, but I do not mind exposing my vulnerability one bit. I still see your smiling face everywhere I go. But then I wonder to myself whether you still love me?

Eternally yours,
Anonymous

Until a year ago, no one knew or understood the real reason Celeste bought the little shop. America had been bogged down in the middle of a costly war and was suffering from rising racial, ethnic, and generational tensions at home. Many people had been refraining from the sort of old fashion leisure time and social interaction the café provided. The entire nation was dismayed and the atmosphere in the 'Big Apple' was no exception. New York was not the city it once was. Somehow, its declining population and rising crime rate had changed it. The city had lost its once undeniable glamour and many small business owners had either gone out of business or fled to the growing surrounding suburbs.

When its previous owners filed for bankruptcy, she'd hinted to family and friends that she might want to buy the café and restore the sentimental attachment it had for many people in the neighborhood. Now that Celeste had spent a small fortune on the purchase and renovations, she still was unsure whether she was doing it to help others or relive her past. But regardless of how much the renovations had cost, she was convinced that eventually, the store would pay for itself. So far, she'd been right. People were coming into the cafe without regard for the war in Asia, civil rights protests, or anti-war marches throughout an entire nation.

Celeste remained seated at the desk with a piece of paper hidden underneath the palms of her hands. When she read the note two weeks ago, she had become distraught and wondered about the possible motives behind such sensitive words. She liked the words, there was no doubt about that. But they had such a heavy sense of sadness and a half-hearted withdrawal from life. Yet, those same words hinted at a continued search for hope. She had always found comfort through these types of notes because they reminded her that love and all its sacrifices were indeed universal. Though, what bothered her most about the note was that its handwriting resembled Francis' handwritten notes he'd written for her many years ago. "Is it possible Francis is in the United States?" she caught herself incredulously thinking. "And if he is, how long has he been here and where is he now?"

Celeste remembered when she read the note for the first time. It was during her usual evening ritual, where she would sit at the desk in her office and ask one of the cafés' staff to bring her the usual hot green tea with lemon. Then, after the young waitress brought the tea, she mentioned in passing, a sort of peculiar man that had come into the café earlier that day.

"He said how happy he was to see the shop still standing after all these years. But he seemed confused when I mentioned the grand opening night, we had three years ago. It seemed like he wasn't around here then. What stood out to me was when he suddenly told me that love is timeless. Then he wrote it down on a note and pinned it on the bulletin board. I can almost hear his soft and sweet voice," the waitress concluded.

Celeste looked at the note again and began to flashback to the first time she read one of Francis' notes. "Love me tomorrow!" it read. And she had gone on to love him with all her heart and with every fiber of her body. All the while, he continued to write her hundreds of short, sweet love notes. They all so romantically expressed his great love and affection for her. Celeste adored that, and everything else, about him: his manners, soft-spoken voice, poetic words, sensational musical talents, loving heart, and undying devotion.

So naturally, Celeste was confused and deeply disappointed, years ago, when Francis insisted that she leave Saranda immediately by ship. Without him. She understood that the situation was dire because of all the conflicts that were happening at the time in that region. Francis was right to be concerned about her safety and well-being. But she couldn't, and still didn't, understand why Francis refused to leave with her. She left southern Albania that August 1941 with tears in her eyes, not realizing that with her she carried a secret about which neither she nor Francis knew.

*****

When she returned home later that summer, Celeste went back to Juilliard to continue her studies of dance in their Fine Arts Department. Over the next few months, she also found time to start saving for their wedding. Except for the obvious situation of him still being in Albania, Celeste was absolutely certain Francis was the man she wanted to spend the rest of her life with.

She would also frequently visit his family's house in Brooklyn, hoping to find him there. But Francis was nowhere in sight. She felt increasingly hopeless after each visit despite friends and family trying to console and encourage her. Nobody really understood how she felt. She missed Francis horribly. Celeste's deep love for him made it difficult to accept the possibility that he might never come back to her.

There was a larger purpose behind her visits, along with her obvious love for him. Four months after her return from Albania, her little secret was becoming a bigger and more visible one to friends and family. The secret she carried within her was their growing unborn child. Celeste gave birth to a beautiful baby daughter, which they had conceived with love during that unforgettable nighttime visit to the Blue Eye. She named her Stephanie. After the birth of her daughter, Celeste had hopelessly continued her visits, but this time not to Francis' family home, but instead to Jonathan's house. She searched, in vain over the years, for a lover and a father. After seven years, her hopeless visits stopped altogether.

Celeste went on to become one of the most talented ballerinas in the world, performing in some of the finest ballet companies around the globe like the Opera National de Paris, the Vienna State Opera, the Royal Danish Theater, the Royal Opera House in London, and the Metropolitan Opera House. With over two-thousand dance performances, she became an instant hit in the world of ballet with sold-out crowds in thirty different countries. But wherever she went, and whenever people applauded her for a sensational performance, Celeste would always search for his face in the audience, hoping Francis was sitting out there somewhere, watching her dance to his music.

For Celeste, the years seemed to pass quickly, and they soon turned to decades. There were times when she tried desperately to forget him, but always to no avail. She would meet other men, but quickly dismissed them and made some excuse. The truth was that no one could take Francis' place in her heart.

***

She was now convinced that the note placed on the café's bulletin board two weeks ago belonged to Francis. Celeste could never forget his unique handwriting. Like so many other things about Francis, it was forever engraved in her mind.

Were these short letters a way for them to reunite again? Was it fate pulling them together? Or was it some random coincidence?

At that moment, Celeste pulled herself out of romantic pondering and back to reality. She stood up from the table and slowly walked to her office. Celeste began rifling through her pile of old records. Then she saw it, dusty and towards the bottom of the stack. Her favorite. One of Billie Holiday's records.

As the old record let out the first crackling sounds, Celeste went to sit down in her chair. When the music finally started playing, her mind once again wandered through time.

***

Francis finished playing the piano piece from "The Dying Swan." He paused for a moment and wondered if he'd made the right decision by leaving the cello behind in Albania. The cello had represented him in every step of his life. It had become synonymous with his real character and sense of identity. He'd never abandoned it before, and now he was wondering if he had pushed away from the very thing that was most important to him throughout his lifetime, his instrument.

Sometimes Francis hated himself for not telling Celeste, right there on the Albanian docks, the real reason he wasn't going with her on the ship that warm summer day in late August 1941. He had tried to give Celeste little hints by saying things like, "I've got to help somebody." But Francis wouldn't give her any more details. Not only for her own safety, but also for the safety of those he was trying to protect. Celeste tried several times to get more information out of him, but he went right on replying, "baby, trust me, I will come and find you later."

After he had walked Celeste to the docks and watched her board the ship, Francis looked on as it slowly disappeared beyond the horizon on the blue waters of the Ionian Sea. Over the years, he had thought about how much those calm waves resembled Celeste's tears as they slowly poured from her eyes.

***

With tired and bloodshot eyes, Francis returned to his cobblestone house where a Jewish couple and their young son had been hiding in the attic for more than a week. Another Albanian family had entrusted their safety to his grandmother, who wholeheartedly accepted to hide them. But Francis refused to allow such dangerously heavy burden to be borne alone by a good-hearted elderly lady like his grandmother. So, he decided to take it upon himself to help the young couple escape certain death. But Francis did not tell Celeste out of fear for her safety. Francis reasoned that the less she knew the safer she would be if detained and questioned. Only Francis knew about the Brokofskys, a family originally from Central Europe, who had come all the way to South Albania after learning about 'besa,' a centuries-old Albanian traditional code to protect guests at all costs. He planned to keep them sheltered in his house until he could secure them forged documents.

Although Germany would not occupy Albania until 1943, there were serious concerns about whether the Italian Fascists would start enacting some anti-Semitic policies on behalf of their Nazi counterparts. Policies similar to, or more aggressive than, the 1938 Italian Racial Laws. However, in many places throughout this small tight-knit country, many Albanians preciously valued their friendships with their fellow Jewish guests and countrymen. Most Albanians chose to protect them from detention, torture, and extermination even at the risk of their lives. Impressively, no Albanian ever turned in any Jews over to the Italian Fascists or even the later German occupying Gestapo. Francis had been one of those good-hearted individuals who helped a loving couple make it safely out of the country and through the war unharmed.

Before the end of the war, Francis was able to purchase forged documents for the couple in order for them to flee the country. He had done so in a spirit of goodwill, knowing that by safeguarding the couple, he was jeopardizing his own life and risked never seeing Celeste again. But for Francis, this young couple had to be saved at all costs. In them, he saw the same unbreakable love he and Celeste possessed for each other.

For the next thirty years, Francis lived with a clear conscience knowing that he'd done something noble by protecting the lives of a family in need during the century's darkest hour. The result of his efforts was rewarding, and he knew he'd done the morally correct thing. But this noble gesture had come with dramatic personal consequences. The price of his clear conscience was the loss of his youth, his freedom, his American values, his love. A love he had allowed to escape at a pivotal point in his life.

As Francis remembered these events from nearly twenty-nine years ago, his attention slowly shifted back to his love for writing short notes. In them, he found a sense of release and a short-lived gratification that lifted the heavy psychological burdens from his mind. Through them, he attempted to console his past and free his emotions.

Yet, Francis had not written a single note in two weeks. Now, more than ever, he needed to write another one. His pinned-up feelings about all the changes in his life since moving back to New York were like a cauldron ready to explode. He decided to drive to Astoria again to visit Café Place. He figured that while there, he would have the opportunity to draw inspiration from a familiar atmosphere and post another note filled with emotional remnants of his past.

Francis got up from the piano and lowered the keyboard cover. He walked out of the study room and headed into his bedroom. There, he rifled through his clothes in his closet. Most of his clothes consisted of pullover polo shirts, long-sleeved dress shirts, and business suits. After shuffling through different outfits, a casual buttoned-down, navy-blue shirt caught his eye. Francis buttoned his shirt and carefully tucked it into the pair of black khaki pants that he'd been wearing throughout the afternoon. Then, he brushed back his graying hair with his hand and covered it underneath his favorite Yankees baseball cap. Francis kissed his mother goodbye and headed out the door.

***

Celeste's mind wandered while Lady Day sang, "I'm a fool to want you." The song's lyrics described a life remarkably close to her own. The passionate lyrics expressed how her life was meaningless without her man. Celeste, like in the song, loved Francis and held true to that love against all odds. In all the years since they had been together, she never lost hope that one day he'd return to her.

The fact that Celeste had stopped going to his house was not entirely her choice. The decision lay mainly with Francis' mother, Anna. She had become extremely discouraged about her son's possible fate while awaiting his unlikely return. Her grief was so great that she became deaf and mute to the outside world. And one day in early December 1941, during one of Celeste's visits to the house, Anna started blaming her for encouraging her only son to visit Albania during unsafe times. At that point, it was obvious to Celeste that Anna was simply looking for anyone to blame for her despair.

Celeste did not know what to make of Anna's outburst or how to react. And although she had felt tempted to explain that it had been Francis' idea to visit his grandmother, she felt compelled to hold her tongue, for she understood that his mother's loss had become too much for her to bear.

Moreover, Celeste had never offered her any details from that fateful August day in 1941. That it was Francis that refused to leave with her. Celeste reasoned that Anna needed to cope with her situation in her own ways. It was not right, in Celeste's mind, to present any excuses while Anna tried to process her grief. Because she knew with unconditional love, such as Anna had for Francis, there were no words or excuses that could properly justify any actions that lead to the loss of a loved one. Celeste let it go, but that night, while driving to her Astoria home, she cried. She wept for the way things had turned out.

All through the years, Celeste regretted her decision not to tell Anna about Stephanie. She had wanted to tell her initially. She knew that it wasn't fair to keep a grandmother in the dark about her granddaughter, especially when the latter was the only connection to a missing son. With that said, Celeste knew that Anna should not be punished for any harsh words which were spoken out of pain.

Despite these feelings, Celeste decided to raise Stephanie by herself, understanding and resigned to the fact that Stephanie would never have a chance to know her father or paternal grandparents. However, she tried to fill that void in Stephanie's life by providing her with all the essentials in life: motherly love, education, a shoulder to cry on, and plenty of together time.

It was during these times that Stephanie would often ask about her father. "Tell me more about daddy," she'd asked Celeste at nine. Celeste would smile and say, "What can I say about your father, he was a saint." "Does that make me the daughter of a saint, mommy?" Stephanie would ask innocently. "Yes, baby," Celeste would hug her and then tickle her endlessly. She was touched and amused by her daughter's numerous questions about him.

Toward the end of the junior year in high school, Celeste helped Stephanie apply to college. They learned about and visited more than a dozen schools, but Columbia, Yale, Harvard, and Georgetown were her favorites. In that exact order. Stephanie's top choice remained Columbia University and getting accepted there was her main priority. Her mother had always told her that her missing father had applied and been accepted there when he was her age. Stephanie felt that going to Columbia would in a way bring her and the memory of her father closer together.

As part of her college application, Stephanie wrote an essay entitled "Pursuing an Old Dream," in which she described her family history and the circumstances surrounding her desire to attend Columbia University. With the help of her mother, Stephanie recounted in detail how her missing father had been accepted to the school at the age of seventeen but never got a chance to attend. She described how he was her source of inspiration to excel academically and apply to Columbia University, so she could complete the path that had been snatched away from her father.

A university dean in his eighties, on the acceptance board, read her inspirational essay and remembered reading a similar one many years prior. When he noticed that both were written by applicants with the same last name, he sent a request to meet with Stephanie in person. The frail dean motioned for her to have a seat and offered her something to drink. Stephanie declined so he asked her the obvious question: "Are you related to a Francis Petrela?" Stephanie, with a torrent of tears welling in her eyes, replied, "That's my daddy."

"Ah, I remember personally endorsing that young man's acceptance and was always looking forward to meeting him. His essay was exceptionally impeccable, daring, and filled with emotions. But he never came. I always wondered what became of him."

Stephanie was accepted into Columbia and four years later graduated top of her class, Magna Cum Laude.

***

Celeste looked at the folded paper in her hand once again. "This is the reason I haven't slept for over two weeks," she thought. Each passing day, she was increasingly convinced that Francis had returned. She wanted desperately to go to Brooklyn and see for herself. And if he had indeed returned, Celeste had so much she wanted to tell him about her life. The most important thing she wanted to tell him was about their daughter.

But if Francis truly had returned to New York, Celeste wondered what would she tell him about herself? Was she to pour out the accumulation of all her suppressed feelings in one night? Was it wise to come out and tell him that she still loved him? That she never stopped doing so? She decided to answer these questions for herself on the way to Brooklyn. For now, she simply wanted to enjoy more old music and let her mind drift in a sea of fond memories for a bit longer.

***

Now it was 5:30 in the afternoon and the Sun was still blazingly hot. As the cab pulled over to the curb on Broadway Avenue, in front of the Café Place, Francis glanced at a man and his young son walking along the sidewalk. The sight of them, lovingly walking hand-in-hand, left him with an empty feeling inside. One of his greatest regrets was that he did not have any children, successors to his family name and legacy. It was a horrible feeling of loss that repeatedly made his chest tighten when he thought about it.

After paying the cab fare, Francis walked along the sidewalk that led to café's main entrance. He stopped at the door for a moment and turned around to glance again at the father and son. Their poignant image together faded as they walked away down Broadway.

Francis was pleased that, due to the ceiling fans turning in unison throughout the café, the air was refreshingly cooler than outside. He also was happy that the café was not too crowded. Only two of the tables were occupied by customers. One waitress was attending to their needs. The other waitress was ringing up something at the bar's cash register with her back to the door.

Francis scanned the café for a suitable space and finally decided to sit at a corner table next to a window. He took out a pen and paper and was about to write when he heard a familiar voice. "Can I take your order?" Francis turned and saw the young waitress that had waited on him a few weeks ago. She looked over and smiled at him with the same warmly welcoming smile she had before.

"A cappuccino and ice-cold water, please."

The young girl was about to walk away.

"Oh, and miss, can you please give me change for this," Francis handed her a dollar bill.

After handing her the bill, he went straight back to his pen and paper. As usual, he paused for a moment, while trying to collect his thoughts. However, before he had a chance to scribble any words, the waitress returned with the coins.

"Ah just in time," he smiled, "maybe a good song will inspire me."

He stood up and walked to the corner of the room to the jukebox, selected a song, and quickly headed back to the table. Francis again began writing.

***

Just then in Celeste's office, another Billie Holiday song started playing on the record player. Celeste began to let her mind drift off again. Through the soothingly hypnotic voice of Billie Holiday, she began to reflect on her past and hoped its happiness was but a prelude to her future. "A savvy woman appreciates her past, understands her present, and builds her future," she remembered her mother once saying.

While Celeste was deeply thinking of her potential future, she noticed that the last song of the record had stopped playing. The music she was hearing in the distance was not coming from her office but from the jukebox in the coffee shop. Who could have picked that song? Who could have been in the mood for Billie Holiday songs this early in the afternoon? Who, from the younger crowd that mainly came into the café, listened to this kind of music nowadays?

Celeste got up from the chair and flipped off the wall switch to the office lights. She closed the door behind her and walked down the short hallway that led to the main floor of the cafe. There she saw a man wearing a baseball cap, his attention seemed intensely directed to the objects on the table. He was scribbling down something on a piece of paper. The man looked up at her as she noticed the trademarked New York Yankees interlocked letters on the front baseball cap. However, the bill of the hat was so low that she could only partially see his eyes. Celeste instantly felt her insides tighten.

Celeste tried to keep calm and outwardly pretend to be unaffected by his brief glance. She headed to the bar to try and confirm his identity with the young waitress. "I'm not sure because I can't see his face clearly with the hat on either," the waitress replied.

Celeste sat near the bar all nervous, with her back to the table. She tried to glance at his reflection through the mirrors behind the bar.

Suddenly, an idea popped into Celeste's head. The jukebox had just finished playing "I'll be seeing you." She got up from the barstool, walked to the jukebox and browsed through some record selections. Celeste slid her coins in the slot and punched in the numbers to the song she wanted. "Heaven, I am in Heaven...," sang the soothingly familiar voices of Ella Fitzgerald and Louis Armstrong in their beautiful rendition of "Cheek to Cheek."

At first, Francis remained unfazed by the music, still drawn to his writings on his piece of paper. This jazzy version of the song began its brief, somewhat different, introduction. But the difference stopped right there, the opening lyrics resonated with his heart's memories and through every cell in his body. Francis looked up towards the jukebox and noticed that the same woman, he had briefly seen minutes ago, was standing there. But now, she was looking directly into his eyes. At that moment, he recognized the resemblance of someone he knew. But who?

Francis stood up from the chair and began to approach her slowly. He suddenly stopped, astounded as he recognized a birthmark beneath her bottom lip. For a while they stared at each other, frozen in their tracks. Here there were.

Celeste Salek, a forty-eight-year-old, successful business owner, once one of the most celebrated young ballerinas in the world, searching for an anonymous writer, baseball enthusiast, and long-lost lover.

Francis Petrela, a 48-year-old emotionally lost political dissident, and aspiring musician surprised late afternoon by the ballerina that had come to dominate his sleepless nights.

Reunion

Now the sunlight streamed in through the windows, illuminating everything in the path of its mesmerizingly radiant light. The rotating ceiling fan did not seem to be having any effect on the heavy heat blanketing the room. . . For them both, their blood felt like it was steaming hot.

They remained still as if held in place by ghost-like memories they had of one another. Twenty-nine years of separation, over three thousand miles apart, thousands of sleepless nights combined between the two of them and it all came down to this. Now only two feet of empty space separated them from one another.

Francis had not uttered a single word. Yet, he felt his palms sweating and muscles tightening up. Celeste began feeling guilty for making this reunion more difficult by playing his favorite song the way she did. Over the years, she had thought it would be easy when time came for them to reunite. But now that the time had finally come, it seemed extremely difficult and somehow inappropriate to say anything. All she could do was try to recognize those familiar, yet mysteriously dark eyes.

Francis immediately removed his cap, exposing his entire face to the yellow sunlight streaming through the windows. Suddenly, Celeste nearly burst into tears as she noticed his flecks of grey that now blended with his brown hair. She moved a little closer. His ridged nose, thin lips, the dreamy, dark brown eyes. The faint scar on his forehead.

Celeste forced a smile, with a thousand questions running through her mind. She wanted her smile to be more natural, but the situation felt so emotionally complex. She did not know what to say, or how to say it. Twenty-nine years apart can do that, she thought to herself. Despite her sudden speechlessness, Celeste still remembered how she would gently caress his face during intimate moments. Now, she meticulously tracked the familiar lines, curves, and angles. Still such an angelic face, she thought to herself.

"Hello, my name is Celeste. It is a pleasure to meet you again." She instantly threw her arms around Francis and held him tight as he remained stiffly unmoved. Almost frozen by the presence of a phantom that had dominated his thoughts and prayers through the years.

Her formal introduction startled him initially. It was the exact one Francis had used when they met at Bohemian Hall. As Celeste hugged him tightly, Francis remembered little pieces of vivid details of that night, like a movie playing in slow-motion on an old fashion 8mm projector. Francis gently moved his arms around her, his eyes welling with tears. He felt the culmination of the pain, love, unachieved dreams, and sudden hope come back. He felt sixteen again. "The pleasure is all mine, Celeste Salek," he stammered.

Celeste heard the tremble in his voice. His soft-spoken eloquence was still present, regardless of the circumstances. The music in his voice, though slightly off-key, pleasantly ran through her mind.

After all these dreadful years, his loving presence engulfed her once again...

Now, old feelings came back to her. Her heart quickened as she remembered memories long since forgotten rush back like a blazing fire. After the first seven years without him, Celeste had tried to move on with her life, and perhaps...

Perhaps, Celeste had thought that her search for him through the years had been useless. Perhaps, she'd become more content with fond memories of the past, rather than continue with hopes of meeting together in the future. And perhaps, she now realized how foolish she'd been for entertaining such thoughts. For she never stopped loving him, never stopped searching for him. In every musical note, in every song, she had seen his face, time and time again. In every word, she had heard his voice, deep and mellow, soft and soothing.

Celeste leaned back to look at his face again. She noticed crow's feet around his eyes, but in the depths of those dark brown eyes, she also saw their once exuberant mysteriousness. In them, she also saw something else, something unfamiliar. She saw pools of tears.

She had never seen tears in his eyes, even as Francis accompanied her to the docks. He had fought back his emotions that day, convinced that they would meet again.

For a while, they stayed frozen. Not uttering a single word. Raw emotions… Neither one anticipated this afternoon, this café, to become their eventual reunion.

Francis gazed at Celeste's vibrant beauty. There was a natural glow to her appearance, one that came with maturity and age. Francis wanted to hug her and kiss her, as he had done during their two-year relationship. But somehow, he hesitated.

There were a thousand things he wanted to say, but none seemed appropriate. His tongue was tied, his thoughts clouded. Finally, Francis blurted out the most natural thing that came to mind. "You look amazing. I didn't recognize you for a moment." Francis said looking resigned and a bit apologetic.

Celeste blushed as tears filled her eyes. She wanted to caress Francis' face to show that she forgave him for not recognizing her. But she withheld from doing so.

They glanced at each other for a while, absorbing the moment in silence. Francis finally sat down slowly at the nearest table, as if he were trying to catch his breath or avoid fainting. For the past ten or fifteen minutes, he had been racing against time while seeing the light of hope at the end of the tunnel.

"How's everything? What are you doing here?"

The question came as a surprise to her. Not that Celeste did not expect it. In her mind, however, this café was the place that would bring them back together, repeatedly.

"I bought this place three years ago," she responded while sitting in a chair next to his.

Francis' now wet eyes bulged in surprise as he looked around the cafe. Celeste had seen that disbelievingly surprised expression on other people's faces, especially right before they'd tried to convince her that buying the place wouldn't be a good idea. She looked back at him wondering what Francis was thinking.

"The idea of this beautiful old place, with all its memories, going out of business bothered me," she said, justifying the reason for such a costly investment.

His mouth suddenly became dry. His heart started pounding so hard, he was sure Celeste could hear it. Francis wasn't sure if this reaction came from being caught by surprise; or perhaps something else. Somehow, he suspected Celeste had another unstated reason for salvaging the place.

"You were always nice like that," he admitted without offering additional comments.

Celeste wasn't certain with his last remark. Is he only trying to be nice? Or is he being genuinely honest.

"I mean I ran the numbers and all, and I figured that it would eventually become profitable," she justified further. Celeste intently looked at Francis, this time searching for his facial expression to either confirm or reject her reasoning.

Francis nodded, though he was unsure whether he did so in approval or simply as a reaction to his utter disbelief. He looked around the cafe and noticed that she had not changed much from its original decor. Remarkably, the newly renovated café closely resembled the old one he remembered. The only changes he recognized were the new placement of the jukebox in the center of the café and the bulletin board. "How long have you been back?" she asked.

Celeste's question brought Francis back to the present, making him realize that now he'd been given a new lifeline.

"It's been a little over a month," he replied.

Francis looked at her with his dark brown eyes. She's probably wondering why it took so long for me to come back, he thought. But despite sensing her curiosity, he did not offer her any additional information.

"How's your family doing?" she asked.

Francis paused for a moment before answering. "Mom is alright. Old and beaten down by all the years of waiting for me." His voice trailed off as he pictured the faces of his father and grandmother in his mind. "Granny died in '43 and my dad in '65."

"I'm so sorry Francis," she replied softly, knowing how much they'd meant to him.

"It's alright," he grimaced, visibly aching over the loss of his loved ones.

"Your family was always loving and kind. You should always remember that" she consoled him.

"Thank you. I know, and I feel blessed to have called them my family," Francis trailed off. "My grandmother never stopped talking about you," he said softly. Words rolling achingly from his tongue while remembering his beloved grandmother.

Celeste glanced away.

Now, he looked at her, trying desperately to read the meaning in her reaction. Francis tried not to make any references to their past. But now that he'd slipped, he was searching her facial expression for some signal of her feelings. To his great relief and satisfaction, she slowly began to smile warmly.

"She was a wonderful lady. Always pleasant. Always said the right thing. She would give me over-the-top compliments even when I didn't deserve them," Celeste replied shyly while looking off into the distance.

Francis looked at Celeste as she looked away. He was still, even after so many years, captivated by her graciousness and elegance, her humble words and regal demeanor.

"Granny did not compliment you only for the sake of it," Francis submitted. "You have always been an incredible woman. You still are. You never cease to amaze people. The passion you have inside has always been special." He paused momentarily and looked around the coffee shop. "And what you've done here tops it all. I am speechless."

Celeste looked at him. He was at a loss for words indeed. Francis hadn't anticipated this. For the last two weeks, he was awed by the touchingly gentle words on the café's bulletin board. He now understood that somehow it had been her passion that brought together these young couples. More than anything, Celeste was a rare individual. She was someone who had tried to reconstruct the atmosphere they had once shared in this old café.

Francis breathed heavily, feeling as if an invisible hand had gripped his chest.

"You were right Celeste. You were always right."

He hesitated for a moment to make sure he did not say anything improper. He looked at her hand. There was no wedding ring on her finger... Suddenly, he felt somewhat freer to speak his mind. He felt a bit more assured this was a sufficiently appropriate time for such a gutsy remark.

"This cafe brings us together time and time again," he said, referring to a quote from the class essay she had written all those years ago. Then he looked away, suddenly unsure if he'd made the right reference or misquoted it after so long.

Celeste smiled broadly. This had been precisely her thought process during the last two weeks since discovering the anonymous note. It was her thought at this precise moment, as well.

"I did not expect you'd remember my essay per verbatim," she replied.

"Things like your essay are what kept me alive over the years."

Her face became blushingly red, as she suddenly imagined the kind of suffering Francis must have endured.

"It was a gift I could never part with," he continued.

Indeed, a gift it was. Francis had taken it with him when visiting Albania. He read it while fighting in the hills, with bullets flying over his head. He kept it close to his heart and soul, and even in his blood.

As Francis and Celeste remained seated, they heard a loud honking sound from outside. Francis looked out the window. The vision of the father and the young child came to life in his mind again. At that moment, he became lost in these images. His gaze grew distant, an expression that Celeste immediately recognized.

"Are you alright?" Celeste's face grimaced with concern as she realized Francis was blankly staring into space as if in a trance.

"Could be better. Could be worse. I thought I'd never see you again," he answered.

Francis wondered whether his somewhat flippant response had sounded convincing. He wasn't sure how much longer he could keep his feelings bottled up. Thankfully, the young waitress came by the table. Her presence took some of the heat away from what could have evolved into a bigger emotional rollercoaster.

"Bring me the usual please," Celeste said.

After the waitress walked away with the orders, Francis smiled. "Let me guess; green tea with lemon?"

Celeste smiled glowingly, but in her mind felt tremendous relief that she was steadily becoming more comfortable around him.

When the waitress came back with their refreshments, Celeste turned her attention to her and said, "Josephine, I'd like to introduce you to a special old friend of mine, Francis."

Francis smiled courteously, but beneath that smile was disappointment that Celeste had referred to him simply as an old friend. Fortunately, he did not have much time to dwell on those feelings, because he noticed such a pleasant expression on the young girl's face.

After the waitress left, Celeste looked at Francis with smiling eyes. "I think she really likes you."

Her voice trailed off for a bit as she remembered, during many early evenings like these, when she'd talk to Josephine for hours about Francis.

"I told Josephine about you a couple of years ago, a few months after I hired her. The funny thing is that, after she noticed you here a few weeks ago, Josephine came to me and mentioned that you might be the kind of guy that I would *finally* marry."

Francis said nothing. She never married, he thought. "So, you knew that I was here?" he asked eyeing her curiously.

"She directed me to a note," Celeste continued softly, her eyes flickering with affection. "It was your handwriting. I could never forget it. But then, I wasn't sure. I mean, after so many years, a part of me really wanted to believe that you were here. That you still thought of me. That you probably came to find me. And your letter was exceptionally heartbreaking. I wanted to believe, trust me. But I did have my doubts because a part of me thought that maybe this was a teasing coincidence. Please, don't be mad. Don't think that I knew for sure. It's so difficult to explain. I am not sure whether you still live in Brooklyn. I mean, do you still live there?"

Francis leaned sideways toward Celeste. He framed her face gently between his hands and looked at her with his mysterious eyes.

"Stop worrying. I am not mad at all. I am just impressed with how brilliant you are. The fact that you went out of your way to read an anonymous note tells me that you are still unique, one of a kind. I am glad to meet you again. I really am!" Francis pressed his lips against the soft skin of her forehead. His heart now was pounding again.

Francis pulled his arms back and they continued drinking cold beverages to fight off the heat of the early evening. The refreshing drinks also provided them with a much-needed break to avoid turning an emotional reunion into a gut-wrenchingly emotional one.

***

Francis spoke about his life in Albania. He gave vivid impressions of the war and fight against the Nazis in the Albanian mountains. The German squads had thunderously marched into the country, while Francis and his comrades would wait for the opportune time to ambush them. They had clashed in some heroic battles.

Once, he had narrowly escaped unscathed with a bullet grazing below his shoulder. Her essay, that he kept folded underneath his shirt, was stained with the blood from this wound. He fought on while still wounded, never abandoning his friends. But none of these sacrifices compared to what would soon follow. "The worst thing was yet to come after the war," he said, "when I became stuck there against my will."

Francis explained how the small country lived under the worst type of political regime after the war ended. It was one thing to fight in a war, hoping to free the region from fascism. But it was a totally different animal to live in a constant state of silent fear. "During my confined existence of thirty years, I longed for simple liberties that we as Americans take for granted."

He told Celeste about Nikolla and his family. Francis recalled how they helped him fill the void in his life. "Despite the fact that they were avid supporters of the government, they never treated me as an outsider," said Francis.

Francis proudly described how he had become a teacher in Albania, always with his love for American jazz in mind. Day after day, he had devoted himself to instilling in young children a passion for music.

Finally, Francis talked about his friendship with Nina, leaving out intimate parts of their relationship. He described her as charming and selfless. Celeste listened intently as Francis described how Nina put her life at risk to help him leave Albania.

To her dismay, Francis offered no explanation of why he wouldn't leave Albania with Celeste that fateful day. But she did not provoke him or initiate any talks about it. Instead, she asked questions about his final moments in Albania.

"Was your escape difficult?"

"Of course. If it were easy, I would have done it years ago. It is not only the final act that is the most crucial. Escaping such an oppressive regime is a whole process that involves many variables. It requires planning, complete trust of others, unfavorable weather conditions…"

"You mean *favorable* conditions?" she spontaneously interrupted.

"No, *unfavorable*. The more unpleasant the weather, the less vigilant the border guards are when guarding the area. They'll probably stay warm inside their booths or vehicles. Sometimes, they're unable to hear things they normally would when the weather is pleasant, and the night is silent and still. But again, who knows? I flirted with the idea of escaping too many times but never had the courage. Luckily, Nina and her boyfriend had the courage for me and gave me a second shot at the life they thought I deserved."

Francis traveled through many Greek provinces, where locals received him warmly and amicably. After months of carefully moving and hiding in Greece, he reached the American Embassy in Athens. Francis was interrogated there for nine months under the suspicion that he might be a secret agent. Shortly thereafter, when the interrogators cleared him, the embassy reestablished his American passport.

As Francis explained the final moments before coming back to the States, Celeste felt great sorrow for him and his restricted ways in life. Pain and a loss of innocence were vividly displayed in his mysterious brown eyes. In his tone, Celeste could hear the naked fury and agitation with the cruelty of the world. Thirty years of deprivation will do that to a person, she thought to herself. But amid all that, Francis had staved off all obstacles before him, now reclaiming his place in the Sun.

Through his recollection of events, Francis did not forget to mention that his heart always remained with his American way of life. For Celeste, a confession like that meant only one thing: that the boyish dreams of his youth were always present in the back of his mind.

Francis abruptly stopped talking. He and Celeste sat in silence looking at each other, perhaps both fully realizing how a random chain of events had brought them back together to this old café. Perhaps, it was God or fate. Or maybe, luck.

Francis inhaled deeply, trying to fully grasp the last twenty-nine years all in one breath. He was trying to find positives, so he could feel better. As he exhaled the air from his lungs, his mind was filling with distant thoughts.

"You know something though…"

"What?" she immediately asked with eyes intensely trying to read his expressions. She was hoping that now Francis would finally reveal the reason for not being able to leave on the ship with her.

"The one thing that kept me going, despite all the freedoms that were taken away, was my job."

"I can imagine. You always loved music," she replied innocently.

"Yeah… but there was much more to it. A lot more." He then trailed off a bit, as she looked at him with growing curiosity. "I loved teaching children. I loved those kids dearly. In them, I saw the children that I always wanted us to have."

The Truth

In that moment of chaos, Celeste did her best to hold a straight face, but she felt as though the ground was trembling beneath her feet. The once talented and graceful ballerina found herself unable to maintain her balance as Francis spoke those words. She now fought some semblance of control.

Amid the rising emotional tensions incurring from their unexpected reunion, Celeste had completely failed to mention their daughter, Stephanie. Not that she had intended to abruptly come right out and say "oh, by the way, we have a daughter." But naturally, she felt, it would have been more appropriate for her to have laid the groundwork beforehand to minimize his inevitable shock.

Celeste asked to be excused for a moment and headed to the restroom. She stood in front of a mirror. There were wrinkles around her wet eyes. She had first noticed the cow's feet some years ago during nights like these when she was reflecting on her youth.

But now, she was standing here in front of the mirror for a different reason, to emotionally absorb what she had witnessed. More than two hours ago, she had seen a ghost reappear from her foggy past. And for her, it had all become mystically surreal a bit too quickly.

Francis had been gone for an awfully long time. She led her life without him by her side. Despite her enormous success as a professional ballerina, she struggled as a young single mother raising a child all by herself. She had tried to be both a mother and a father to their daughter. She had undergone all the sacrifices of a single parent. She'd done so proudly and without any complaints.

Celeste turned on the faucet and let the water run for a while over her hands. Then she splashed the cool water on her now refreshed face. She looked at herself in the mirror, hoping that the sprinkles would also calm her nerves down. "Now, it's the moment of truth," she murmured under her breath, "time to tell Francis about our daughter."

Celeste wiped her face with a paper towel. Then she turned off the faucet, flipped off the lights, and headed out of the restroom, down the hallway, and into the dining area of the cafe.

Francis remained seated, anxiously anticipating her return from the restroom. In the meantime, he was growing concerned, for reasons he could not understand. He thought that Celeste's mixed reactions had something to do with him using the wrong choice of words.

Now he closely watched her again while she sat down across from him at the table. Although Celeste was trying her best to hide her feelings, Francis knew that something wasn't right.

"There is something that I'd like to tell you," Celeste submitted, briefly glancing at him, then nervously looking away.

"What is it?" Francis asked while rolling a torn piece of paper between his fingertips.

Celeste looked around, desperately trying to buy more time. Then suddenly, her eyes became fixed on a corner of the café.

"Do you remember when we use to sit there all the time?" she said while motioning with her head. "That's where I sat when I wrote my school essay."

For some reason, Francis could tell she was stalling for time. However, he decided to go along with it and respond in ways that might make her feel more comfortable.

"We were in love." He paused briefly and remembered that day vividly in his mind as if he had rehearsed it over and over. "You told me that I was the main person in your life," he replied with a broad smile on his face.

"You were very important to me," she reaffirmed.

"I think I understood that much by reading it," Francis chuckled nervously. "I always considered myself lucky around you."

Celeste blushed and smiled but then seemed to drift away again. Francis looked straight at her and began to recognize her expression as a form of hesitation and reluctance about something.

"You can tell me whatever is on your mind," Francis said, attempting to calm her.

Celeste looked around and realized that the fresh air might have a calming effect on her anxiety. This was not going to be easy.

"Do you think we could go for a walk?" she countered with slight hesitation. "Like old times…"

Francis nodded.

The two of them walked out the door.

***

Now it was 8:20 pm and the evening sky had become beautifully silver. Somewhere off in the distance, the Sun still illuminated the farthest edge of the sky. The air was humid but much cooler than it had been three hours ago.

As they walked along Broadway, they decided to turn right on one of the quiet side streets. For a while, there was silence between them as Celeste tried to contemplate the possible scenarios of her impending admission. No clear way of broaching the topic came to her mind. Instead, she tried to divert attention to small talk, gesturing to certain vacated premises on the block and recalling the families that used to live there.

Francis recognized her poorly disguised apprehension.

"Did you ask me to walk with you, so we can reminisce about old families?" he asked gently, foreseeing the emotional magnitude of the situation. Whatever she is thinking, Francis thought, it has got to be quite difficult for her. "Talk to me. What's going on?"

"I am being silly, aren't I?" she asked in a humble way.

"No, you're not. I know this day has been as difficult for you as it has for me."

She looked at him and took a deep breath. Finally, the moment of truth, she thought.

"I have a daughter…"

Although Celeste was speaking in a normal pattern, for Francis her last word seemed to have dragged on for too long. He felt as if someone was tearing his insides out. But he had no feelings of blame for Celeste. He didn't expect her to shut herself to other men over the years. He knew that life had separated them for way too long.

"I'm happy for you," he trailed.

Again, she blushingly looked away, wishing that the truth wasn't so damned hard. Her eyes were brimming with tears as she wiped the corners. Celeste then turned to Francis and looked directly into his eyes.

"Do you remember when I said that you were the main guy in my life?"

He nodded.

"I meant it. You were the only guy. You were always the only person in my life…" She then paused for a moment. "In our lives," she added cautiously.

Francis felt the invisible hand squeezing his chest again, leaving him breathless.

"What are you trying to tell me?" His eyes trying desperately to read her face. "Whose lives?"

She swiftly broke eye contact and looked at the floor nervously sensing the moment when the whole truth would emerge.

"Mine…hers."

Now Francis once again felt the invisible hand gripping his chest tighter, repeatedly, as he waited for Celeste's answer. She lifted her head back up and they looked at each other.

"We have a daughter," she stammered. "Her name is Stephanie."

Francis grabbed the metal bar along a bricked wall for support. For some reason, the short wall and the sidewalk suddenly seemed to be moving. He leaned against the railing to regain his equilibrium as he tried to absorb the shocking news.

Francis began breathing heavily and felt his heart pounding in his chest. He looked at the pavement and closed his eyes a couple of times, thinking this was a dream. But each time that Francis opened his eyes, he and Celeste were in the same spot looking at each other. Francis began breathing deeply and slowly to pace his sprinting emotions.

Breathe in...

Breathe out…

In and out…

Francis remained still. His posture resembled the prolific image of a statue that stared back at its observer with emotionless eyes. He simply allowed every thought, every feeling to slowly move through the unfamiliar places in his mind. Yet, his gaze remained unchangingly distant.

"Francis are you alright?"

Her question might have briefly brought Francis back to the present, but he was still trapped in waves of shock. Waves from which he could no longer escape.

Celeste awaited his words, which never came. Naturally, many questions were running through his mind as he was struck in disbelief. So instead, she decided to volunteer more information.

"She lives in London," said Celeste. After a brief pause, she smiled at Francis. "She is tall and beautiful. She is warm and possesses a big heart. She is amicable and fits right in with everyone. Her words and wisdom are immeasurable. When she talks, she reminds me of you and your passions."

Celeste sat and watched Francis bury his face in the palms of his hands. They stood there momentarily, for what seemed like a long time. Celeste watched his shoulders shuddering while he wept.

Phone call

Later at night, Francis dialed her number. "I will come for you, I promise," he remembered telling her that summer day in Saranda. In his heart, he knew that this was the time when that promise had finally been fulfilled.

"Is it too late?" Francis asked, unsure if his phone call had awakened her.

"No," Celeste responded softly. "Actually, I'm glad that you called. I can't sleep. There are so many things that I want to talk to you about."

She did her best to keep an assertive tone while she spoke.

Francis could sense a bit of tension in her voice while listening to her talk. "Sure, what is on your mind?"

"Somehow, I still cannot believe that you're back. And we spoke of so many things that we have missed in each other's lives. At least for my part, I have a lot more explaining to do." Celeste's mind immediately drifted to the moment when she told him about Stephanie.

"Celeste, I'm incredibly happy to see you again. I'm not expecting you to explain anything. All that matters to me is that you're alright." His voice sounded soothing and comforting.

She knew that Francis was not asking for an explanation. But she *did* want to tell him more and felt that the night had not been long enough to do so properly. "I want to see you again. Is that ok with you?" Celeste said breathlessly while feeling her insides twisting with anxious anticipation of what his response might be.

Francis could almost hear her breathing and understood how difficult the night must have been for her.

"I want to see you too. I am hoping that we can take some time to get to know each other again." By this time, Francis felt his grip tighten around the phone.

She felt relieved with how easy Francis was making it for her. This is how she always remembered him. Patient, mature, considerate, and kind.

"Come with me to Lake George." Francis felt instant pressure, not knowing what her response might be after all these years.

"What's at Lake George?" she asked.

"There's an old house. I haven't had a chance to go yet. I figured this is a perfect time."

"Great," she replied. "Let's meet there."

Morning Contemplation

Friday. It was almost ten o'clock in the morning. Francis had finished drying himself off after a long shower. He had been up for almost four hours, and as usual worked on his garden in front of his Brooklyn house. He removed weeds and watered the tulips that he had planted over the course of the last several days. He always took great pride in the quality of his work and made sure that what had been fixed thus far in the garden remained pristine throughout.

After drying off, Francis put on a pair of khaki pants and a light cashmere V-neck shirt. From the small breakfast table, he grabbed the cup of coffee which his mother had prepared. He sat in the rocking chair and gently rocked back and forth, occasionally lifting the edge of the cup to his lips. The aroma of the Brazilian coffee left him with a fresh and sweet taste in his mouth. It was by far his favorite part of the morning.

While sipping the coffee, he flipped through the pages of the newspaper, largely disengaged from the news articles in it. Most of the articles were about crimes in New York, domestic violence, and the war in Vietnam.

After finishing his coffee and with the rest of the day still ahead of him, Francis sank into his usual morning thoughts about life, its purpose and his love for Celeste.

Life had been no legendary path by any stretch of the imagination. Francis had realized it long ago; from the moment his thoughts of a possible escape became a mere disillusion. There were no excuses, other than fear, which could possibly justify why he waited so long, to break free from something which he stood opposed.

To say that he had not been on the brink of escape several times would be deceptive or a huge understatement at best. But there was always that fear factor. The fear of being caught, the fear of not finding what he left behind, the fear of failing. There was always the fear of something…

Now Francis' heart was pounding loudly in his chest. It had started the night before. He knew that these palpitations were happening because now he was coming face to face with his fear. And that fear was consuming him. The fear of being exposed to a different reality… Perhaps he'd left Albania too late... He had not been there for their daughter. He'd never seen her grow up; never seen her at her first recital; never taken her little precious infant body and protect it in his arms.

Celeste had not told anyone about Stephanie. Francis was perplexed by such huge omission. However, he was not upset with Celeste, nor was he annoyed with Anna. They both had acted naturally within the context of their emotional situations and from the confine of their own perspectives.

He remembered in a conversation with his mother a few weeks prior: she had blamed young Celeste for encouraging him to travel unnecessarily during unsafe times. The now elderly lady regretted her choice of harsh words.

"My son, the hurt of a mother is unbearable, implacable, and immeasurable on any scale when it comes to losing a child. Celeste was a sweet girl and I know she loved you dearly because I could see the pain in her eyes too. I saw the same pain in her eyes that I felt in my heart. But as a mother, I thought that only I was supposed to grieve you. That it was only my pain, not hers. And all these years, I knew I was selfish for having her excluded from our family. You must believe me that, at the height of my dilemma, I did not know what I was doing or saying. And I hurt that sweet girl in the process." As Anna concluded this conversation, she burst out in tears.

Francis hugged and kissed her. And at one point, as Anna's head lay on his chest, he said, "Mom, the beating of this heart I owe to you.

You and pops together worked hard so that I wouldn't have to miss out on anything."

As Francis remembered this conversation from a few weeks back, he thought of all the things that were in store for him now. Life was too short. "No more useless analysis," he promised himself, "only focus on what is in store for me going forward."

The night before, they decided to go away to Lake George, somewhere that provided them with an escape from everyday life. The old house at Lake George was the perfect place. A backdrop for the cellist and his lifelong swan.

He now picked up the phone to let her know that he was heading to Lake George.

The Test of Life

Celeste walked around the living room with her eyes glued to the floor. The morning was hotter than usual, and the Sun poured through the open windows. The blazing heat had produced perspiration droplets on her forehead. The ceiling fan did not help either. Not that it mattered to her.

She seemed too busy counting the steps that covered the distance from one wall to the other. One, two, three, four... She counted to fifty-nine. It seemed as if she was not really into the routine. She seldom paid attention to the floor and sometimes miscounted the steps. Then she'd start over.

Hundreds of thoughts were running through her mind. The thoughts that rushed her this morning equivocated a swinging pendulum. On one hand, she wanted to tell him that she'd waited for what felt like an eternity to be with him. On the other, she wanted to apologize for not telling his parents about Stephanie.

Celeste could have easily reconciled with Anna. As a young lady, however, Celeste had always been a proud individual who took other people's words at face value. So, she never really pressed the issue of coming to good terms with Anna.

There was something else though evolving in Celeste's thought process over the years. This one for more personal reasons. She was convinced that if Francis returned one day, he would follow one of two courses of action: either he would romantically scour the city in search of Celeste or he would simply discard her.

Whichever course he'd follow, she wanted him to do it for the right reasons. If Francis came looking for her, he'd have to do it for love, not based on the obligatory premise of having a child. So, she made an affirmative decision that she'd be the first person to tell him about their daughter. No matter what! For that to happen, it meant only one thing. That he had to come looking for Celeste first. This was the 'test of life.'

The 'test of life' did not portray her as a selfish person. Everyone who knew Celeste recognized her graciousness, her pure and loving heart, her sacrifice, and complete devotion. At the height of her career, as a prominent dancer, she always searched for his face in the audience with longing and pain.

She didn't have to feel this way. But she made a choice. Her soul belonged to none other than Francis. So, when she met other guys, she never really made love to them. To her, no one was as kind, tolerant, and understanding. No one possessed his thoughts and class. No one could ever replace him.

Essentially, her only mistake was that she tried to compare everyone to him. In her mind, she had idealized his image as something pure and holy. An image impossible to duplicate.

The restoration of Café Place, bringing the shop back to life after its near extinction, was her final attempt to keep hopes alive. She restored it to recreate magic found only in places like this. She wanted to return meaning back to a place that had been abandoned, so that young people could enjoy it the way she did decades before.

After counting and miscounting the steps across the floor, she sat near the window. She opened it and stuck her right arm out as the sunlight warmly caressed her hand.

Celeste touched her old necklace. She whispered, "I will never forget you, not tomorrow, not forever," referring to the tiny inscription inside the heart locket.

Celeste began to unconsciously touch her breasts through her baby blue blouse. She imagined Francis touching her gently. All these years, she had been yearning for him, dreaming of him, imagining what it would be like for their bodies to merge again.

She got up from near the window and walked towards the kitchen. There was a pot of boiling hot water on the stove. As she was about to pour the water into a cup, Celeste heard the phone ring. She looked at the clock on the wall. Ten-fifteen.

Lake George

They decided to meet up nearby the Million Dollar Beach. It was Celeste's idea to meet there. Going far away from home can often create loving and long-lasting memories. This idea certainly played a part in her decision when she'd thought of possible locations, they could meet along Lake George. The beach had been her first and only option. It was the only place she remembered from her lone previous trip to the lake.

Francis arrived there a little earlier than Celeste. He had managed to take one of Jonathan's old cars. And despite its engine's annoying sounds, the car probably afforded him with one of the most scenic rides of his life. The place that stood most in his mind was the beautiful scenery as he approached the tiny hamlets before the surroundings of Albany and Lake George. He had been driving for about three to three and a half hours when he came to a stretch of road with only hills and rocks on either side. The distant hills were blanketed with countless shades of green which were typical in early Autumn. As he drove closer to the hills, he realized that there were also acres of pine and maple trees. Most of them were green too, but with various specks of yellow, red, and orange interwoven.

This lovely scenery satisfied his creatively artistic side, as he drove along the highway. He was traveling with the car's windows rolled down, alternating between 60 and 70 miles per hour. The whispers of the early Autumn winds were blowing uncharacteristically across the open fields in a way Francis had never experienced. Briefly, the music of Louis Armstrong was drowned by nature's mystical sounds in the distance. Also, by the sounds of the car's engine and tires as Francis drove on the highway. The fresh smell of countryside's pine and maple trees seemed to fill not only every inch of the car but also imbued his very soul.

Upon arriving at the tourist area of the town, Francis decided to do a little food shopping for their weekend ahead. He stopped at the corner, where there was a large grocery store and picked up some freshly made Italian bread, potatoes, green peppers, eggplants, and other delicacies.

After placing the bags of groceries in the trunk, Francis drove along the street adjacent to a picturesque walkway that led to the Million Dollar Beach. Once there, he parked the car next to an old antique shop and decided to walk along the scenic cobblestone pathway. Along the path, there were small flower beds, quaint kiosks, and antique lamp style posts.

He was standing next to a low water fountain when he first noticed several horse carriages like those that one might expect to find on the cover of an old magazine or book. The calming vision of the horse carriages, coming and going, painted in their same original colors, seemed like a scene taken straight out of the nineteenth century America. The horses were now being led away by their owners, who every so often entertained their patrons with stories about this area of Lake George.

Francis thought about taking one of the rides. But instead, he decided to observe from a distance. As he watched carriages taking their usual shifts and bystanders awaiting their turn, he paid close attention to patrons' reaction at the end of their rides. Simple expressions spoke thousands of words.

Out of all the observations, Francis became fascinated by the sight of a father and child walking side by side. Even more so, by the story of this little beach that stretched along a small portion of the shoreline.

"Daddy, I did not know that the Million Dollar Beach is called so because that's how much it cost to have the sand out there," the young child, not more than twelve years old, yelled out to his father.

The father did not say much but simply nodded his head reaffirming that the beach was indeed built on a million-dollar investment several years before.

Francis let his mind wander a little longer as he watched several tourists pass by, a man with his pants rolled up to his knees and a fishing pole in his hands, a young couple hugging beneath one of the antique lamp posts, a young male embracing his sweetheart from behind as they looked out towards the lake, and several more horse carriages changing shifts.

One hour or so passed before Celeste arrived at the arranged meeting place. It was now around five or six by the time she made it there.

"How was the ride," Francis asked.

"It was absolutely breathtaking," Celeste answered with a tender voice.

They soon sat outside a café, not far from the Million Dollar Beach, and ordered their usual refreshments.

Tall and slender, Celeste looked about ten years younger than her age. Traveling through the natural beauty of the preceding towns and witnessing the seemingly simple lives of the people along the way, revealed a different way of life. For her, it was an overflowing abundance of beautiful surroundings and a breath of fresh air. Away from the noisy complexities and endless responsibilities in the big city. She now had an enormous smile on her face as though she finally remembered how to relax and enjoy herself.

The last two weeks, since she'd suspected him of being the man posting the anonymous note, had been emotionally overwhelming. It had taken away a great deal of energy. Now Celeste had forgotten all the sleepless nights that led up to this point.

Celeste looked stunning; Francis remembered thinking. And indeed, she did. Traveling through the lush rustic landscapes had also given her confidence and mental calmness that things were finally starting to take shape. The psychological burden was slowly being lifted. A man could appreciate a woman with confidence, whose smile radiates every aspect of life.

Francis also noticed the tension from the night before vanishing from her face. After the waitress brought along their favorite refreshments, Francis and Celeste stayed frozen until she finally sipped her cup of tea.

"It's so peaceful here," Francis said, his voice still resembling Italian virtuoso Enrico Caruso.

"I know. I came up here only once in my life, several years ago. Sometimes I am upset with myself for not coming more often."

She trailed off after she spoke, knowing that her hectically busy routine in New York City was to blame for all sorts of simple things like this she'd missed in life.

Celeste looked off into space with sort of a distant gaze. "The simple things in life," she remembered young Francis' voice saying thirty years ago as they explored nature. When life was indeed much simpler for them both.

She did not intend to dwell on the past. But during their long separation, her life had felt like a disjointedly fragmented existence. Celeste was learning that the last thirty years had been as tormenting for him as they had been for her. And though, in Francis, she saw hope for their immediate future, she also discovered changes in him she hadn't noticed when they first saw each other.

Last night, Celeste had found it rather difficult to recognize Francis' face. The bill of his Yankee cap had hidden his eyes and most of his face. But now, seeing his face in broad daylight, each time their eyes met, she could see the toll his survival had taken. After all, one can understand a lot about a person only by looking in their eyes, the true reflection of the inner being.

And it was a moment like this, under the skies of Lake George, which made their years of longing for one another worthwhile. It was during times like these when the Sun shined so artfully over the blue surface of the lake.

Francis tried to figure out what she was looking at by following her gaze. His eyes fell instantly upon the magnificent, seemingly infinite, body of water. Small boats' white sails floated atop. The lake, calm and radiant, appeared limitless except for where it met the low hills. The place where the lake and hills met, which was the beginning of the Adirondack Mountain range, seemed to signal the entrance to a lush new world.

"What is it?" He asked, though he already knew the answer only by following the direction of her gaze.

"How could anyone ever get tired of this?" Celeste asked rhetorically. "How can one ever get enough of anything?" He murmured in yet another rhetorical question.

She immediately looked at him. He turned the chair so that his body could face her completely.

"There is something that I have to tell you." He paused for a second, wanting to think critically about what he intended to say.

"What is it?"

Francis looked away and did not reply for a moment. He found it rather difficult to directly speak about things that involved them.

"I never thought I'd see you again. My life during the last thirty years, as I explained to you last evening, was empty. I mean not completely empty, but it was filled with pain and suffering. And I tried to make sense of that pain, and no matter how hard I tried not to at first, I finally resolved myself to simply accept the misfortunes. Amid some of the pain, I saw a little light by embracing my surroundings. The positive in all this was that in my struggle, I found an Albanian family which took me in as their own."

Francis paused for a moment as a lump rose in his throat. He looked away again, this time for several minutes. In the silence, Celeste felt deep sorrow for him and attempted to offer him words of understanding.

"I know this must be difficult for you. You don't have to talk about it if you don't want to."

"Not that I don't want to. But I don't know how to say it. I thought it would be easier but now I realize that no matter how I say it, it will sound as if I am making excuses for myself."

"Excuses? What excuses?"

"Excuses for not being there for you, excuses for not being there for our daughter, excuses for not being together as we had always dreamed."

"Francis, you don't have to explain yourself. It is not like you knew that I was carrying a baby. Neither one of us knew."

"Yeah, but that's still not an excuse for not having been a part of your life all these years."

"Francis, you did not plan on being stuck in southern Albania. There were forces way out of your control. It is alright. I understand. You really don't have to explain yourself."

"But I have to… I want to…" He looked away again, this time realizing how much things had changed since her departure from Albania. "Would you believe me if I said that I never wanted to let you go that day on the boat?"

Something inside her changed as scenes from that fateful day appeared before her eyes. She swallowed hard, trying to downplay the emotional effects of his last question.

"I know you did not want to let me go. But you said that things were becoming worse by the day and that you wanted me to get out of harm's way." Celeste was on the verge of tears by the time she finished her sentence. Her mind had taken her back to every emotion of that moment at the docks as if she were right there again.

"I know, I said that. And I meant every single word. I was not trying to make any excuses then. I promise. I swear on the souls of my loved ones."

"It is alright. You don't have to promise or swear on anything."

"I'm not having this conversation with you to explain why I wanted you out of harm's way. The real purpose is mainly to answer the question of why I didn't get on the boat with you, even though it's apparent I could have easily done so."

Celeste nodded in reluctant approval and looked down. In all her life, that had always been the one question daunting her. But again, she did not want to force the issue and all she could say to him was "It is alright. You don't have to tell me."

"Celeste, I never stopped loving you. I loved you with all my heart before you left the Albanian port aboard that ship, and I never stopped loving you for one moment since then."

Celeste hung her head low.

"Please don't hang your head. I am begging you."

"What do you expect me to say, Francis? That all is forgotten. Here I am trying to stay strong and tell you that it is alright, that you don't have to justify yourself. But deep down inside, my desire for you to explain yourself is as strong as the pain that your absence caused me over the years. And I know that it is selfish of me to ask you to explain yourself because I know you had your own pain to deal with after the war…" Celeste paused and looked sternly at him, her eyes filled with tears. "All I wanted us to do today was enjoy ourselves. Nothing else mattered. That's all I wanted to do. Be with you today. That's all I ever wanted to do my entire life. To be with you. Like the way we were a long time ago. Alright?"

Francis grabbed Celeste's hand firmly and looked right through her tears. The same tears that she had shed when he sent her off from the shores of southern Albania.

"Why didn't you come with me?" She burst into more tears, her voice now sounding helpless.

Francis hesitated and looked at her hands, no ring in sight. He was sad for all the pain he'd caused Celeste. He was sadder about her life. Their lives. Everything on hold for some noble cause. That nobility had subtracted a great constant from the complex equation of life. The most crucial constant of all, love. The type of love that, once lost, most likely would never be reclaimed.

While watching Celeste shed so many tears, Francis felt his entire existence sinking. He pulled his hand away from hers and buried his head in his hands.

"What have I done? What have I done to us?" Francis kept repeating to himself.

Celeste's tears kept pouring down while his head hung in a gesture of intense humiliation. Perhaps he was embarrassed that he'd never had the opportunity to tell her the true reason he had been unable to leave with her on that boat. And if he told her the truth now, what difference would it make? At this point though, his confession didn't matter. It did not matter because he owed Celeste the truth, now more than ever. And not only to her, but Francis knew he also owed it to himself. No matter how that truth might be perceived, excuse or no excuse, it was bound to set him free.

"If I were to tell you why I didn't follow you that day, would it make a difference now?"

"Yes, it would make all the difference!" Celeste abruptly exclaimed as her tears kept pouring. She then grabbed a napkin to wipe her tears.

Francis looked at her without whispering a word as if the gravity of the situation had severed his vocal cords. Before he could say a word, Celeste placed her napkin down on the table.

"And you know why? Because even though I'm extremely happy to see you again, I need to know that what we had was real."

"Oh, Celeste…" Francis sighed softly.

His sigh sounded so helplessly regretful it could have made the coldest heart feel the sorrowful sincerity in his voice. Francis suddenly stood up from the chair, knelt before Celeste, and wrapped his arms around her in a tight embrace. Everything happened so quickly that Celeste had no time to react.

"Our love was everything I had. Our love was what had me looking into space. And that empty space was no longer empty because I would see your face and feel your presence."

He then placed his head on her lap, not caring about what pedestrians might think of this public gesture.

Celeste put her hand softly over his head and slowly caressed his hair. She was shocked by his open show of emotions.

"I did not follow you that day because a man and woman were waiting at my grandmother's house in the attic. Along with their little boy. They were waiting there to be rescued. They were Jewish, Celeste. They were Jewish, and I couldn't leave them alone at the mercy of the State in those painfully difficult times. Germans did not come to Albania until '43; however, we were uncertain if the Italians would enact any anti-Semitic laws on behalf of their German counterparts around 1941. Do you understand what I am trying to tell you? That our lives were put on hold, that our love was tested for so many years. All of that was for two strangers who I barely knew. I couldn't leave them alone to die. I couldn't."

As he finished the last sentences, he moved his head from her lap and looked up at her. His eyes filled with tears.

She wiped the warm tears from his eyes, as they ran, seemingly endless down his cheeks. Celeste looked at him with such profound admiration. Through the clear lens of her love and melancholy, her eyes now beheld the man she once knew; the righteous man who was tirelessly selfless in his efforts to help others. The man who had once, long ago, captured her heart with his principled ideals.

"After I helped them out of harm's way, it was too late for me," he went on explaining. "There was a blockade as the war became more intense and I could no longer find a way to leave. Compounding the situation, my grandmother was still alive and extremely sick. She was an old fragile lady in the middle of a nasty war. Everything was so complicated."

"Now, it is too late," he continued. "Too late!"

Celeste caressed his face. This time, she forced herself not to cry, wanting to be strong for him; wanting to be a shoulder for him to subdue his pain.

They did not say much after his confession. They stood there a little longer before they headed out to Bolton Landing.

The Old House

From far away, they could see the Sun's rays stretching over the majestic Adirondack Mountains. When they made a final turn at a curve in the road, they drove along a narrow unpaved, downhill road. The road was lined with tall and ancient trees apparently old enough to have been there before the first Europeans set foot on the continent.

When the car came to a complete stop, they saw a huge house in the stone style. This property, unlike the group of houses they saw two or three miles back, was in a secluded part of Bolton Landing. Bolton Landing, located to the north of the lake, was characteristically quieter and more affluent than some of the other villages surrounding Lake George.

No matter where one went. Tourists and residents alike. From Lake George Village, Bolton Landing, Ticonderoga Settlement, or Millionaire's Row. They were all taken aback by the magnificent and breath-taking views of the lake. To sum up the picturesque site in the words of President Thomas Jefferson in a letter to his daughter, "the lake possessed the most beautiful view, formed by the contours of the mountains which formed a basin, finely interspersed with islands, its water limpid as crystal, and the mountainsides with rich groves down to the water edge."

The carved stones of the house reminded Francis of his house in Saranda. This one, however, with two floors instead of one, was both grander in size and in impeccable condition. He had been at this property once, over thirty-six years ago, when his aunt invited the entire family to celebrate young Francis' twelfth birthday. So, he vaguely remembered some details in the house's interior.

After Celeste got out of the car, she watched Francis walk away carrying the groceries. In his khaki pants and cashmere V-neck shirt, he almost looked like the seventeen-year-old she remembered. Despite his graying hair, she thought, he looked as good as the first day she'd ever laid eyes on him.

She watched Francis until he disappeared beyond the front door. Unwilling to let go of him, Celeste closed her eyes. She wanted to keep his image in her mind for eternity.

Celeste raised her arms gently in the air and spun slowly. She took quick, short breaths to inhale both the fresh air and their fresh start. She now knew that her life would have a new beginning.

She loved moments like these, moments where dreams and aspirations rode on the back of new beginnings. For her, everything that had been revealed in the afternoon, despite the tears and the agony, confirmed that Francis loved her through and through. After his heartfelt revelation, she realized that it was not his heart – but his logic – that sent her away.

"Are you alright?" She heard him say from a distance.

"I think so," Celeste softly responded while noticing Francis' head propped from behind the door frame.

He thought he might have heard her say something else, but her tone was as faint as the early Autumn breeze.

"Are you staying there all evening?"

"I don't know," she smiled slyly. "Should I?"

"I'd definitely answer that question for you. But unfortunately, I am the one asking the question."

"Well in that case, what kind of question is that?"

"It doesn't hurt for a gentleman to ask," Francis answered playfully.

"And a gentleman should always invite the lady properly to the doorstep." She replied loudly again, still trying to hold in her laughter.

Francis moved away from the door and went swiftly to Celeste. He then lined himself up next to her and held his elbow out. "I am sorry. I forgot the formalities."

Celeste burst out laughing, this time placing a hand over her mouth.

"Are you going to leave me hanging here ma'am?"

"No, sir! I would never do such an inhumane thing." She held on to his hand and followed him as he led her toward the house.

As they passed through the doorway, Francis turned around swiftly and shut the door behind him. "The more inhumane thing would have been if you had stood out there while my stomach was growling. I am going to prepare us something to eat."

Francis started walking toward the living room and through the kitchen, Celeste right behind him. He leaned slightly forward to gather the groceries and placed them on top of the kitchen counter. She watched him curiously again, this time wondering whether he had learned to cook out of necessity or out of pure desire.

As he unpacked the last of the groceries, she noticed his muscle tone through his shirt. In that respect, he still resembled his younger version, athletic and fit. He looked great. Even after thirty years. For a second, it appeared all the years had been undone right in front of her eyes.

Francis picked a couple of eggplants and started to wash them in the sink. He then peeled an onion and cleaned it quickly with water so that the odor could not burn his eyes. He also washed red peppers, basil leaves, parsley leaves, and garlic. His hands were fast and yet flawless. Their swift motion reminded Celeste of the old times when Francis had played the cello.

"Do you still play?"

Francis looked up at her, still unsure whether he'd heard her correctly while washing the vegetables.

"I don't know," he replied, shrugging his shoulders while looking down at the faucet. "What do you mean?"

"The cello!" she answered gently. "Do you still play it?"

"I don't even remember what cello sounds like anymore."

Francis turned off the faucet and drained the water from the last bunch of parsley he was holding.

Celeste looked at him flabbergasted while paying special attention to his facial expressions. She wasn't sure whether that last comment was some sort of a joke.

He quickly glanced at her while lining up the now cleaned vegetables on the counter.

"I stopped playing maybe six or seven years ago. They started to use my name and my music to advance their political propaganda."

"Who is 'they'?"

"The people who made unilateral life-changing decisions for the rest of us."

Celeste was beginning to be a little confused. She was not catching up quickly enough to the conversation. Francis had failed to mention the night before that he'd once been a favorite among the Albanian upper command.

"I was discovered at the Albanian Academy of the Fine Arts after the war ended. At first, I decided to play because I found an escape from my miserable life. When I played, people cheered me on. I found a new life and a new meaning."

Francis smiled slightly at the memory of the audiences applauding him after each performance. A brief silence. But then, in the silence, his mind began to wander to images of contradicting thoughts and feelings of sadness.

"And though I was stuck in Albania against my will, I thought at least I can make the most of it by trying to find my happiness, or whatever was left of it, within captivity through the hearts and minds of the people. That's the life that I chose until they started to use my name. The people who represented everything that I could not stand."

By his tone, Celeste got the sense whatever was going through Francis' mind had to be quite emotionally difficult for him. The emotions he was feeling had to be somewhat like those stirred by the challenges she had had in her life. Celeste's own struggles in the past started to resurface again. They made her feel empty inside… lonely. Before her mind could begin dwelling on such negative thoughts, she quickly leaned over the counter and changed the subject.

"Can I help you with something?"

"No. Everything's alright. Thanks though," Francis answered while briefly looking over his shoulder and continuing to cut the onion into little pieces. "This is going to take at least an hour though. You're more than welcomed to stay here. If you want though, you can also look around the house."

"It would be great to do that." She answered while walking away from him. "I'll also get my stuff out of the car. Did you need me to get anything of yours out of the car?"

"No. I got everything already."

After Celeste put her things away, she took a tour around the house. Nothing about it seemed out of the ordinary. The house had a living room, three bathrooms, and four bedrooms with their bedsheets neatly folded. It was a typical lake house, which was designed to provide people with an escape from their everyday lives.

She also walked outside and explored around the house, where she noticed an old boat atop a rusty portage carrier. Celeste also saw chopped wood which appeared to have been there since the previous winter. She heard a bird cooing and immediately looked in the direction of the sound. In that direction, she saw a small house about one-hundred feet away. An unfurled Canadian flag on a flagpole was protruding from above one of the upper floor's window frames.

About thirty minutes passed before Celeste returned to the kitchen. Francis had already finished prepping the stuffed eggplants. They were stuffed with vegetables, rice, and ground beef, placed inside a long pan. The oven was set to two-hundred-and-fifty degrees with the eggplants inside slowly frying. The smell pleasantly teased Celeste's growing appetite.

"That smell is so familiar," she said.

"Stuffed eggplants," Francis replied briefly, as he opened the oven to check on the food's progress.

"Didn't you bring some to my house once?"

Francis paused for a moment to think. How could she remember such a small detail from so long ago? But with Celeste, nothing should be a surprise. Celeste always remembered things like that because she paid close attention to detail.

"Nobody makes them better than my grandmother used to make them," Francis responded with a nostalgic gaze on his face.

Celeste looked at him curiously because she understood that time had taken a great toll on his soul. She and Francis began setting the table together.

In less than ten minutes, everything was ready. He brought out two bottles of beer, opened them and sat at the table. The chair wobbled a little, perhaps because its legs were unsteady.

"Here's to our reunion," Francis picked up his bottle and made a toast.

Those words resonated so mightily that for a moment Celeste forgot to pick up her bottle. "Here's to us," she wanted to say.

She enjoyed the taste of this style of cooking. The meal was both healthy and delicious. As she picked through the salad with her fork, Celeste noted how beautifully placed the parsley and the small tomatoes were in the salad bowl. It was as beautiful as a work of art.

"It's been a long time since I've enjoyed a meal like this," she said.

"I am glad that you liked it," responded Francis while removing plates and glasses from the table.

He returned after he'd finished cleaning and sat down again in the chair.

They were silent for a moment. By now, Celeste had shed any doubts she had since he came back in her life. Any questions that she had, any doubts and any disappointments in life... they had all gone away.

She had accepted that the pain that his absence inflicted would remain until she died. Celeste had accepted this as a reality. She was resolved to this only if she could preserve Francis' image – the way that she remembered him. But now, Celeste wouldn't have to deal with the pain of remembering their time together. She also wouldn't have to cry herself to sleep and hope for a night dreaming of him. Now Francis was hers again, back in her life as if he'd never left.

"What's it like?" he broke the silence.

"What's what like?" she asked.

"What's like to have a child?"

"It's the most wonderful feeling in the world. At first, when I missed my period, I had a feeling. As months went by, another life take form within me. It was our child that helped me take my mind off many things."

"What is she like?"

"She is smart, beautiful... intelligent. She's gifted with knowledge... beyond description. She's an idealist like you."

"You mean… she's stubborn like me?" Francis asked playfully.

"She made one of her teachers reconsider the structural fairness of the American criminal justice system. She told him that political partisanship should have no place in the judicial rulings and what is just can only be determined by the people themselves."

"Ah… in that respect, she is like her old man."

They both laughed. Francis laughed louder though. He was happy that his daughter took matters of justice seriously, the way that he would have. The necessity for a fair criminal justice system was no more evident than his experience in Albania. The only difference is that in Albania, people that thought like his daughter would have been immediately killed.

"Francis, I also have a confession to make."

"What is it," Francis looked at Celeste curiously.

"As you know, I never told your parents about Stephanie."

Francis looked at her. He'd thought about it in the morning and was a bit hurt by it. No matter what the circumstances, he thought, she could have at least sent them a postcard.

"It's alright, Celeste. You don't have to explain. I know all about it."

'I know all about it.' To Celeste, this wording was like being lost in a foreign country and someone giving directions in a foreign language. She knew what Francis was trying to say but didn't understand the words. She kind of got the gist but didn't know where his words might lead.

"I do not think that what I did was fair," she said.

"Celeste, I already told my mother about Stephanie. She does not blame you for not telling her but blames herself for kicking you out. You can ask her yourself when we are back in Brooklyn."

"I am sorry. I am really sorry," Celeste lowered her eyes apologetically.

"Hey now… Don't be so hard on yourself," Francis looked at her compassionately.

"You were always nice like that," Celeste said while looking up at him.

He looked at her not really understanding what she meant. She sensed his confusion. "You never blamed me for anything. You were never hard on me. You always gave me guidance. You made excuses for my faults."

"I loved you like a madman. What else was there for me to do," Francis grinned.

Not long after, they went out on the porch, Francis sat in one of the rocking chairs and Celeste in the other. The Sun was completely out of the sky, and now the moon ruled in its place with unquestionable authority. The sound of the distant cricket, the falling of the Autumn leaves, the silence of the sleeping lake…

"Say something," she said to him.

Francis began speaking in a soft voice like he had to Nikolla during one of those long nights in southern Albania. He spoke of his life as a musician when he was at the height of success. Before it had all come crashing down. Before he'd found out that his music was being used for political reasons.

He recounted how he couldn't bear to live a lie. Music embodied everything and every aspect of life. Yet, music transcended all life's mundane facets. Francis had found music in the obvious places: piano, cello, and gramophone. But he also explored it in nature, baseball, literature, and in love; the grandest place of all. There was musical beauty attached to all enjoyable things in life. Without a doubt, the type of music that he loved and appreciated was in and for anything but propaganda.

"Anything but propaganda!"

The words played over and over in her mind while he continued speaking. The sky grew darker, and the moon rose higher as if to say to them, "I'm here for the rest of the night."

Francis looked at his watch and saw that it was getting late. He had enjoyed talking to Celeste and now wondered what she'd thought about his decision to abandon his career as a cellist.

"That's deep! Your decision had to have been difficult. I know how much you loved that cello."

He looked at Celeste and she returned his gaze. For a moment, her facial expression seemed to say, "I told you! You are an idealist."

Francis got up, went inside the house, and filled the teapot with water. He came back a few minutes later with two cups of hot tea.

"Why did you not tell me about them?" She asked.

"About whom?"

"About the family that you were trying to help in Albania. Why did you send me away so abruptly without letting me know? I would have understood."

"I didn't think it would have worked out well if I had told you. I mean, it was tough. At first, I thought you, or anyone else, knowing about the couple would be unsafe. But later, thinking about how compassionate and caring you were, and still are, I realized I had to be the assertive one and make a decision for both of us."

"I would have understood, Francis!" She again exclaimed. "This wasn't solely your decision to make."

"The situation was becoming more difficult," he went on to explain with unflappable logic. "The war was worsening by the minute. Had I told you the real reason for staying, you would have ended up convincing me, one way or another, to let you stay. And I knew that I could not afford to do that. I know I may have seemed cold and thoughtless in that moment of separation. If it hurt and haunted you since then, which I know it may have, I am so sorry. Because as much as

I wanted to help them to a safe passage, I also wanted to make sure the person I loved most was out of harm's way and back in America where she belonged."

"Yeah… It makes sense. But can I let you in on one little secret?"

"Sure," Francis replied.

"When you sent me off, I thought that your feelings for me had changed. I thought that you'd done it to be single and pursue other women."

"Never in my life would I ever do that," he sighed. "I would have told you so, if that were the case."

He looked at her one more time, before letting out another sigh: "Never!"

Celeste looked down at the quilt wrapped around her legs. She was ashamed of how she'd thought then. Francis had never been the type of person to lie or deceive her in that way. Indeed, the boy she'd known so long ago would never have done such a thing. He was too great of an idealist, too noble of a person to treat others as cheap and interchangeable objects.

Francis rocked gently, back and forth, in the rocking chair with his eyes closed. He knew that he'd begun getting lost in his thoughts…and drowning in his memories…

It was typical for a dreamer to repeatedly do so.

They stayed on the porch a little longer until eventually deciding to call it a night.

A New Friend, A Familiar Sound

Full of hopes for the future and dreams of the past, Francis fell asleep on the porch that night. He dreamt of meeting Celeste at Bohemian Hall.

In his dream, they saw each other for the first time. He, the cellist and she, the swan fluttering its wings. They hadn't known each other before that night. But as Francis melodically played the cello and Celeste gracefully moved her arms and legs, they made eye contact. At that moment, they realized that they were made for each other. After this realization, they walked along a foggy street. They didn't know where they were going. Yet, they had enough trust to stay by each other's side. And so, they kept on walking.

After Francis woke up and found himself on the porch, he thought about the dream. It had been filled with somewhat dramatic effects. These effects must mean that there was a deeper meaning to the dream. For example, he, being a cellist, and she, a swan, could mean that Celeste always danced to his type of music... or perhaps dance to his love. And their walk along a foggy street could mean their trust would help them persevere through life's many unknowns.

He wished the dream had continued a little longer despite the slight differences from their actual meeting at the Bohemian Hall. He wanted to see where the dream would take them at the end.

Francis, having woken up in the middle of the night and discovered himself on the porch, went inside the house and slept comfortably in one of the guests' rooms.

He woke up early the next morning, having wanted to go for a ride to the nearby mountains. He stretched out his arms above his head, part of his regular morning ritual. The staccato sounds of woodpeckers, the refreshing smell of fresh air, and the leaves rustling beneath the whispering morning breeze had long since been forgotten treats of this place. The even more distinctive sound was the soothingly gentle coos of doves, a rare bird in this area of Lake George.

Francis got up from bed and walked along the finished wooden floors. He intended to familiarize himself again with the old lake house. It was one of those settings that had left him with a lasting impression thirty-six years ago.

The house was built in the late nineteenth century and renovated five years ago with a portion of Jonathan's savings. Jonathan's wife was an only child and when her father passed away, she became the sole heir of the luxurious property.

Julia had initially wanted to sell the place. She missed her father terribly and wanted to part ways with anything that reminded her of him. But Jonathan had persuaded her otherwise.

Francis saw a closet at the end of a hallway. He walked to it and opened the door. He was shocked to find a brand-new cello with a note attached to it that said: "Welcome Back."

He smiled broadly. Jonathan, once again, never ceased to exceed expectations. Promptly, Francis decided to give the new cello a try. The exquisite instrument produced lovely old familiar sounds. He'd missed the one left behind in southern Albania although this one was quite immaculate. While playing, Francis felt a sense of revival and renewal coursing throughout his body.

"Mozart and Beethoven never die," he thought to himself.

And how could they? As long as there were people like Francis, musical greats never go away.

An Oak Tree of Dreams

Francis and Celeste stood in the middle of a calmingly isolated woodland, captivated by nature and its infinite aesthetic resources. In front of them, stretched about two miles of water, a view that extended to the base of the distant mountains. The sky now was darkish blue with only a few specks of rolling clouds, dispersing behind the mountains in the distant horizon. The Sun illuminated only one side of the lake. On the left, the blue nuances of the water reflected the rich groves along the lake.

Celeste walked for a few steps and took a deep breath. The air was fresh and clean. She then tilted her head to the sky, put her arms up gently, closed her eyes, and spun around slowly.

"What are you thinking?" Francis asked her while standing only a few steps behind her.

"You," was what she wanted to say. "This is beautiful," she instead answered while facing the lake.

Francis watched her, as she answered, and was pleasantly surprised with her appreciation of the scenery.

"Yes indeed," he stated while not taking his eyes off her and marveling at her sensual figure. Her supple appearance momentarily left him breathless.

Celeste felt the heat of his glare and immediately turned to look at him. Francis remained unmoved. His broad shoulders. His firm chest underneath a tight V-neck shirt. Sculpted pelvis. He looked fantastic. She realized that something had changed inside of her in the past two nights.

Though she tried not to admit it to herself, during their recent reunion, the thought of him peeking at her body from time to time had aroused her.

"Do you really think so?" She asked provocatively, unsure if she was briefly transforming back into an adolescent.

"It is without a doubt a beautiful place." He reassured her, quickly looking away from the intensity of her gaze as if suddenly struck with a feeling of embarrassment.

Celeste believed him, sensing the deep sincerity in his voice. She believed him because she could somehow see in him the young man that she remembered from the Bohemian Hall. Reserved and timid. Frozen in his tracks.

He painstakingly removed sticks and small rocks, clearing and flattening the ground, not far from the lake's shoreline. From the basket, Francis took out a thin cotton blanket and laid it, nearly perfectly, on the ground. Celeste helped him, taking out the loaves of bread and various types of cheeses from the basket, and placing them on porcelain plates. She then opened the jar of pickled olives and spread them on the plates. Francis uncorked the wine bottle and poured the red wine into the glasses. Their picnic spread was nothing spectacular, but special enough to create a beautiful evening of enjoying the lovely views of Lake George.

After finishing some of the little food preparations, Francis excused himself and disappeared into the woods. He returned a short time later with a few logs and placed them near their little picnic area. He repeated this trip two more times until convinced there were enough for a fire that could last an entire evening.

Francis briefly glanced at Celeste sitting on the picnic blanket and could not help but think of how beautiful she looked underneath the evening sky.

He piled several logs slightly diagonal then did his best to coax a fire, first with dried barks, sticks, and whatever he was able to find. Francis poked the fire a few times to make sure the logs started burning sufficiently. Once he got the fire burning well, he sat near Celeste and made a toast for them to have more times like these.

After they took the first sips of wine, she sighed and slightly leaned her head back.

"What is it?" Francis asked, gleefully anticipating her enjoyment.

"I told you that this is beautiful right?" Celeste rhetorically asked before taking another sip from the wine glass.

"It is beautiful. One of my favorite scenic stops in this entire area..." Francis wasn't sure how convincing he sounded though. The last time he'd been here was at the age of twelve.

Celeste became briefly distracted before looking at him again. "I am glad that you're here with me," he continued.

She saw him smile and shyly look away. Francis stood up and bent down in front of the fire. She looked at him and all the details she'd missed only moments ago. Celeste could see his triceps flex as he fed wood into the fire. The muscular definition in his back and shoulders looked as if Michelangelo himself had sculpted it.

Francis slightly poked the burning logs with a stick.

"Why do you say that?" she asked, fishing for more.

He quickly turned his head.

"'Cuz I am happy," he paused. "This moment reminds me of all the times we spent together."

She smiled warmly before sipping more wine from the glass.

"Can I ask you something?" she said while he continued feeding fresh logs to the fire.

"Anything," he said.

"What is it that you remember the most about our times together?"

"Everything!" he answered innocently.

Francis smiled, knowing how cheesy his answer sounded. He started walking toward Celeste and sat down beside her.

"Well. If you had to pick the most memorable moment, which one would it be?"

"The night we walked together after your performance at Bohemian Hall."

"Mine too!" she exclaimed. "It was a turning point for me."

He smiled. He got up and looked in the direction of an old tree. "That tree carries a story of its own. Which is one of the reasons I brought you here today."

"What do you mean?" confusion surfacing on her face.

Francis stood up and walked to the oak tree. He examined it for a moment, trying to remember every inch by using his photographic memory. Celeste curiously watched him and was tempted to interrupt him with questions. But she remained silent.

He reached into the deep, dark hollow of the old oak tree. Where is it? Is it here? He shifted his hand in different directions and felt moss on his fingertips. No, that's not it. Finally, his hand felt something familiar, and he pulled it slowly from the hollow. An object completely covered with mud. Francis wiped the mud off to see if it was what he remembered. But it was nothing but a plain piece of a lifeless wood.

He extended his hand deep into the hollow again, like he had reached down under the loose floorboards to pull out the old gramophone when craving American music in Albania. Habits never die. Where are you? Francis remembered that he had wrapped it in a piece of a cloth when placing it there during the summer he turned twelve.

"Francis are you alright?" Celeste asked, glancing at him curiously.

"I can't find it. But I am almost there," he answered. "Ah…" He paused.

He then turned to Celeste carefully holding an object. Francis caressingly wiped away the mud. The item was wrapped in a small piece of cloth and tied together tightly with shoelaces. He gently untied the shoelace, unwrapped the mysterious object from the stained fabric, and intensely stared at it. It was a large piece of dried bark that a young Francis had peeled away from a tree that summer while visiting Lake George. With his fingertips, he lovingly caressed the letters carved into it and felt, with each touch, all the years since melt away.

"What is it?" Celeste asked, with a thousand other questions in her mind.

Francis looked at her with his typically mysterious eyes, still holding this relic of his youth in his hands. He extended his arm with the piece of bark resting in the upturned palm of his right hand and gestured for Celeste to discover it on her own accord.

She walked to him, took the piece of bark in her hand, and read the inscription. Celeste stood completely still with her eyes staring at the letters of her name carved in the wood.

"When did you do this?"

"The summer when we first met," he explained to her. "That is when it all started for me, my first feelings for you. And I could not help but carve your name somewhere. If I am not mistaken, I did this a few weeks after you fell off your bicycle and cut your knee."

"I remember cutting my knee. I cried. You tended to me and told me that everything would be alright." She trailed off momentarily and looked away with her eyes flickering." You always had a way of calming me down."

Francis moved close to her and wrapped her tightly in his protective arms. Celeste held him, never wanting to let him go. They stayed that way for a while. The scene resembling all the hundreds of times they had held each other under the sky so many years ago. The touch they both had been longing for during all the interim years.

"Do you know something though?" She asked while moving away to make enough distance between them that they weren't touching. "I fell from the bike that day because I was trying to do a wheelie like you used to. It was silly to think that an eleven-year-old girl could do that. I was trying to impress you."

"Impress me?" He asked while walking towards the shore to wash the dried dirt from his hands. Francis rubbed his palms together briskly, removing any mud residue, and then splashed water on his face, washing away the sweat from his forehead.

"I knew you always did wheelies on your bike to show off. And I wanted to do the same thing…" Celeste's voice trailed off again briefly, but she almost instantly brought her attention back to the present. "I wanted to do it because I thought that I had a crush on you too."

"Really? The ironic part is that none of us said anything. We were way too young to have that kind of courage." He explained standing on the shore.

The calm waters softly touched his feet. His mind began to wander off to the summer of 1935. It was during that summer vacation when, at a young age, he had developed a deep appreciation for nature's beauty and all it had to offer.

As Francis enjoyed the gentle waters kissing the bottoms of his feet, he turned to Celeste, looked into her eyes, and smiled broadly without saying a word.

"It feels so right to see you smile," she said innocently, then reciprocated with a wide smile of her own.

"Well, it feels like heaven seeing you smile back with those radiant eyes," he replied in a soft tone. He looked into her eyes like a poet attempting to paint a beautiful woman with the stroke of his words. "All these years have passed, and you have not lost the glamour that comes with such immense beauty."

Upon hearing his words, Celeste almost gave in to the urgent feeling to look away. Instead, she lovingly gazed at Francis with her hazel eyes. She was deeply flattered.

The scenery behind seemed to be frozen in place still like a picturesque oil painting on a wooden canvas. "What are you thinking?" She broke the brief silence, realizing that Francis was doing a lot more than smiling. That broad prolonged smile had always betrayed his inner thoughts of carnal comfort between them.

"This reminds me of the Blue Eye. You were standing by the edge of the water like I am now. You looked me in the eyes and asked me to make a wish."

"I remember that" Celeste replied.

"You were always outgoing, playful and spontaneous. And when you turned to me saying those words, your face looked so beautifully innocent, but your body appeared so lustfully sensuous in that long sexy baby-blue dress."

This time Celeste could not help but look away. Francis' description of that day, nearly thirty years ago, made her remember the erotic details of when they passionately made love in Albania underneath the ancient oak tree. Suddenly, for the first time in very long time, Celeste felt a wave of warm tingling sensations wash over her inner thighs. These private places she had considered nearly sacredly forbidden to anyone else since that day in southern Albania. She now wondered whether Francis noticed her now erect nipples through her thin blouse.

Despite her growing sexual desire, Celeste tried her best to maintain control over her emotions. Instead, she slowly walked away and sat down on the picnic blanket. Francis followed her there and sat beside her.

"Unbelievable," sighed Celeste. "It seems not that long ago we were only a couple of kids. Madly and deeply in love."

"I think about those times all the time and although they happened in the distant past, they are as clear in my mind and heart as if they happened yesterday."

"Do you remember the first time we kissed?"

"Of course!" Francis sighed with a naughty chuckle underneath his breath.

"I was so nervous then. I knew we were taking a chance since we barely knew each other." Despite Celeste now pretending to organize the spoons and forks on top of the cotton tablecloth, Francis could see she was nervously trembling.

"I thought I was the nervous wreck back then," he joked, attempting to lighten the mood between them thick with memories.

Francis placed his hand on hers and moved it slowly across her skin. She quickly looked at him and smiled, but then looked away.

"How did it feel when we kissed?" He asked her curiously.

"I felt nervous of course. But then that anxious feeling transformed into happiness. I was so glad when you kissed me back. It was a mix of emotions…"

Before Celeste even had a chance to finish her sentence, Francis abruptly leaned forward without notice, his lips softly meeting her warm plump mouth. Initially, Celeste's eyes remained open, a result of being caught off guard by the kiss. But then, she closed her eyes as their tongues passionately touched, danced, and curled. Irregular movements at first, until finally adjusting and moving in sync with each other. Each movement superseding the last in vigor and passion. Kisses so deeply sensual even Picasso would be unable to depict it in his abstracts… A kiss so moist that even the petals of the most beautiful flower soaked in a morning dew would envy.

When they stopped, Francis leaned back slowly, not far, but enough to focus in on her dreamy eyes specked with the reflection of the burning fire next to them. While leaning on his left arm, his right hand slowly caressed the soft skin of her face. Celeste slowly moved her face against the soft touch of his warm caress. A touch she had craved for so long.

"Did it feel anything like that?" He asked, captivated by both the culminating passion of their moist kiss and the bottomless depths of her hazel eyes.

Celeste nodded as gracefully as a sparrow. She ran her fingers through his hair and pulled him closer. With her eyes closed, she kissed him. Their deeply passionate, wet kissing went on for quite a while longer there in the fire's light.

Francis looked at her with his captivatingly mysterious eyes. He ran his fingers through Celeste's hair while gently kissing her forehead, lips, chin, and neck. He then nibbled her ear as she reached underneath his shirt to caress his chest and back. His moist lips and tongue consumed her with an inexplicable wave of emotion which slowly coursed through her entire body.

Celeste tilted her head to better expose her neck, enabling him to kiss her gently as she unbuttoned his shirt. When she had finished completely unbuttoning the shirt, she again sensuously rubbed his taut chest. Her hands felt the warm moisture of his sweat.

Francis kissed her lips as his hands touched her breasts over her thin blouse. He could feel her erect nipples. Even though she was forty-eight, her breasts were as beautiful to his touch as they had ever been.

They briefly parted lips. He took off his shirt and stood there with his broad shoulder and muscular chest. Celeste looked at his physique with tenderness and admiration. The taut definition of his chest reminded her of the rugged mountains they had visited of Northern Albania. She kissed his chest and stomach while softly running her fingers along his back. In her mind, she wanted to capture this one moment to make up for all the time that they had missed together.

Francis affectionately caressed her soft cheeks. Celeste raised her arms as he slowly lifted the t-shirt over her head and gently kissed and licked her shoulder, tasting her supple skin as he carelessly threw the shirt aside. Celeste, now bare-breasted and wearing only a skirt, stood in front of him, softly illuminated by the firelight.

Francis moved his face close to her breasts and lightly kissed her now engorged nipples. As his tongue glided across Celeste's areolas, she sighed in ecstasy, her entire body now engulfed in a wave of intense pleasure. His warm tongue continued to explore her breasts, traveling slowly down to her belly, her body writhing in rapturous euphoria.

Celeste, now a boiling cauldron of elation, urgently unzipped his jeans, reaching to gently grab his hot, firm manhood. He unbuckled his belt and let the jeans fall while groaning with bliss as Celeste slowly stroked him. She looked into his eyes, quietly moaning in anticipation of their bodies becoming one, and unfasten the buttons of her skirt. Francis, now hungrily kissing her succulent lips, tried to help by reaching around her waist. He unzipped the skirt and pulled it down off her shapely hips. Then, they both hurriedly removed their underwear and, once completely nude, paused to lovingly admire the beauty of each other's nakedness. Frozen still, but wild with the eagerness of what was to come.

Celeste laid down on the blanket and Francis crawled over to her, moving above her and more passionately kissing her delicious lips. He kissed and licked down to her breasts as she moaned again. She longed desperately for his teasing to stop. She hungered to feel him deep inside her. That they both be transported to that euphoric place they had been long ago.

Francis slowly lowered his hips between her warm thighs, and they finally became one. He thrust into her with rhythmic tenderness while grabbing her hips and feeling her body's moist reception. Celeste moaned aloud with each thrust; her arms welcomingly wrapped around his muscular chest. He moved gently at first, wanting to please her with every stroke. As she felt the approaching orgasmic culmination of her carnal pleasure, she dug her fingernails into his sinewy shoulders.

Francis knew her tight grip showed her desire for him to thrust faster and deeper. He began pushing his manhood into her with forceful passion, kissing and licking her neck with every stroke. With each thrust,

Celeste felt her blissful excitement steadily building. They freed all their hot sexual passion, not for a second holding back. Their lovemaking was both lovingly gentle and intensely wild. Both emotions combining to create a moment of blissful ecstasy greater than the sum of each individual feeling. Neither Francis nor Celeste felt their pleasure was less than the other. Both were rewarded at their passion's climax with an orgasmic feeling that matched their last explosive lovemaking years ago at the Blue Eye.

The firewood was still burning, and the sky was dark. The moonlight smiled down at them and the stars seemed to have formed their timeless pattern just for the two of them. There lie two beautiful bodies with a fire burning bright, like their passionate longing for each other for all those years. Like two ancient Hellenic sculptures, all the meticulous curves of their bodies were illuminated as if they had become favored among the Greek Gods in this perfectly starry night.

She then lay next to him and placed her head on his chest. She heard his heart loudly beating like it never had before. It was a heart that had carried a torch for her since Francis had first set eyes on her. A heart plagued for three decades with painful longing. Yet, a selfless heart because Francis realized over the years that life's greatest gift was those same painful memories. Yes, they had inflicted him with thousands of sleepless nights, but they also had given him hope of one day reuniting with Celeste

"Look," she exclaimed. "Lady Day!"

"I'll be seeing you in all the old familiar places that this heart of mine embraces, all day through…"

Before Francis had a chance to say the first few lines from the song, Celeste leaned towards him, gazed in his eyes, and said in a whisper soft as a midnight breeze, "I love you, Francis. I love you more than anything in the world. I never stopped loving you. And nothing will ever stop me from continuing to doing so!"

He looked at Celeste and caressed her face. His gaze was grateful and appreciative. Grateful because he could see in her eyes that she was sincere, and appreciative because she meant everything in the world to him.

A Fateful Dream

Celeste made breakfast while Francis slept in bed. They spent the entire night, and a good portion of the early morning, on the shore making love. Even after returning to the lake house hours later, she again threw her arms around Francis, becoming one with him again, as they continued lovingly copulating. They had been consumed by their passionate love, a love that had been missing from their lives since before the bombing of Pearl Harbor.

Celeste placed the breakfast tray on top of the wooden counter and sat in the chair next to the table. She picked up the fork but realized that she was not hungry. Instead, she drifted into memories of her life. Specifically, when friends kept telling her it would be best to forget Francis and move on with her life.

What stood out most in Celeste's mind was a conversation with her mother, seven years after she had returned from Albania.

"Do you think you will ever let him go," Lynn had asked seeing Celeste seated near the window.

"What are you talking about?" Celeste said attempting to play it off.

"I am talking about the ghost that you await every time you sit there staring like it will create some sort of a miracle."

"Mom! I don't understand why you talk this way. He will return one day. Of that, I am sure. He is not a ghost…"

"He is a ghost, Celeste. For more than seven years I have watched you cry yourself to sleep. Enough is enough! You have one beautiful child that is his. Cherish that. Embrace it and move on with your life. All your friends are married and have families. But you, you have nothing because this thing goes on and on."

"I have tried mom. Believe me. I have. You think it's easy. But it's not. Imagine having the love of your life taken away. Imagine bringing to life the fruit of that love, knowing that he cannot be there to watch her grow. Imagine having a child ask for her father every day. How is that supposed to make me feel? I sit here, waiting hopelessly, knowing that no matter what I do will never ease the pain, nor answer the thousands of questions that still linger in my mind. All I have now is hope. Hope that he will come and take away all my hurt and bring back my happiness."

As Celeste remembered their conversation, piecing her memories together in a mosaic, she understood it was that specific conversation which had ignited a shift in her attitude. She became more practical when realizing her mother's advice rang true. A truth that Celeste was unable to see because a world without Francis had been unthinkable. Eventually, she broke out of her shell and moved on with her life. She pursued her passion for dancing more vigorously. She went out with friends to social gatherings, sometimes meeting guys. The truth her mother told her had somehow been liberating. It had allowed her to accept the world for what it was, rather than what she wanted it to be.

By no means did she forget Francis after that conversation. That would have been impossible. Otherwise, she wouldn't have been compelled to search for him in the audience after each ballet performance. She wouldn't have been obligated to restore the coffee shop so that romantic couples would have a place to call home. If she had forgotten him, she wouldn't have felt Francis' presence close all those years or have felt like the world had trembled beneath her feet when they finally reunited.

It had been a few weeks after a conversation with her mother, when she began to think about the Test of Life. One of the reasons Celeste decided to keep Stephanie's identity secret was to ensure that if Francis returned, it would be because of his unconditional love and not a sense of paternal obligation. Her 'Test of Life' also required that she should not give her heart to another, despite being socially active. After all, it would not be considered a true test of unconditional love if it did not involve obligations for them both. She knew that for this commitment to work, they both would have to withstand life's trials.

She smiled, knowing now that they had triumphed over all the obstacles life had thrown their way. It was a small note two weeks ago that led towards their reunion. She lept with joy, realizing that Francis was there with her now to stay forever. The thought of him being back made her long wait for him over the years all worth it.

Celeste got up from the chair and walked across the hardwood floors that led to the spacious living room. She went through the hallway, walked up the stairs, and slowly opened the bedroom door to see if Francis was still sleeping. She slowly poked her head in the door. There he was, the man of her dreams (and now of her reality) lying flat on his back, underneath the cotton bedsheets. He looked so peaceful sleeping and she did not want to disturb him.

She turned away to close the door, but just as she was about to close the door, she heard Francis mumble something. He made a low muttering noise at first, but his words became louder and more distinctive. At first, Celeste thought she had to have been hearing things, so she opened the door slightly to see for herself.

Francis was turning his head left and right repeatedly, with his eyes shut. He was murmuring incomprehensibly, with distinct words only becoming audible once she moved closer. "No! Please! No! Don't go!" he exclaimed as he was having a nightmare.

She touched his forehead and felt the excessive sweat dripping down his face. Francis opened his eyes and sat up, breathing heavily. He felt Celeste's arms around him as she slowly placed her head on his shoulder. His few hours of tormented sleep had left him feeling extremely lonely.

"Are you alright?" Celeste whispered as she lay her head on his shoulder.

"I don't know," answered Francis with a hesitant voice, his pitch low and steady.

"Do you need anything?" She asked, obviously concerned with what had suddenly transpired.

"I don't know," he replied, his eyes horrified from what he had seen in his dream. "Although I know I should know, I don't understand why I don't."

She lifted her head and looked at him confused. Celeste knew that asking him to elaborate might make matters worse. So, she let the topic go and told him she'd go downstairs and prepare some tea for him.

After she left the room, Francis sat on the edge of the bed as sweat poured from his face. He could not understand why, even though things were going well with their reunion, his nightmare had been identical to those he had in southern Albania. They had tormented him and always left him feeling empty in his heart and soul.

In his dream, Francis was at Yankee Stadium, walking from first base toward home plate. The stadium was crowded with people from the past, with a tall umpire behind home plate. For a second, Francis stopped dead in his tracks and picked up his baseball bat. He laid it on his shoulder like he had done in his younger days. The day was bright and seemed promising, with only a few clouds mostly dispersing in the baby blue sky.

The umpire stood several feet away from the batter's box and waited for Francis to step up to home plate. When Francis finally reached it, he came face to face with a tall man, who then removed his umpire's mask. Francis froze momentarily, shaking his head in disbelief. "Dad?" Francis' voice was weak and trembling and his eyes brimming with tears.

His father Luke, an elderly man with grey hair wrinkled face and Dowager's hump on his back, moved his lips, but Francis could barely hear him say, "Welcome home son." Francis followed his father's eyes curiously as he turned his head to look.

There was a young woman, seated in one of the seats, about thirty rows behind the home team dugout. A little girl stood beside her.

From afar, Francis was struck by something about the woman's presence. He wanted to get closer. She was wearing a red dress with a shawl wrapped around her neck, her long brunette hair laying effortlessly over her shoulders. The woman stood up, grabbed the little girl's hand and turned to walk away. She walked up the aisle between the boxes on the main level. Francis dropped the bat in the dirt as he recognized something familiar in her posture and the way that she walked. He quickly hopped over the dugout and followed her up the aisle, making sure not to let her out of his sight.

As he passed each section of seats, he saw himself running through fragments of old familiar places - Coney Island boardwalks, Bohemian Hall, Café Place, Astoria Park.

The woman turned the corner at the end of the long aisle as Francis began to pick up the pace and try to catch up with her. He noticed, once he too turned the corner, that the little girl was no longer beside the woman. She had vanished. Suddenly, people appeared in front of him, forcing Francis to brush aggressively against both young and old to keep up with the woman. He relentlessly tracked her movement, despite his legs aching, perhaps realizing he also was racing, not merely to catch up to the woman, but also against time and fate.

After finally catching up with her, Francis placed his hand on her shoulder. Instantly, she turned around to face him. He nearly lost his balance.

Celeste.

Now she was wearing a black gown and their surroundings had changed dramatically from the crowded stands of Yankee Stadium to the shores of Saranda. Celeste stood in front of him as he pleaded with her to leave Albania. She stared at him without saying a single word, teardrops trailing down her cheeks. Then she lowered the black lace veil which had been covering her face. She turned and solemnly walked down the pier which led to the small boat. As she boarded the boat,

Francis tried calling out to Celeste to say that he loved her, but he was inexplicably unable to speak a single word. The boat traveled away from the shore along the dark blue waters, as Francis stood on the dock, watching his dream and future slip away.

When he awoke, the nightmare had left him feeling completely hopeless. He absolutely loved her, but the dream of her wearing the black gown and veil made him worry that things between them would never be the same. During their thirty-year separation, Francis not only missed her love and tenderness but also missed out on all the many events in her life. To Francis, all the anecdotes she told him about her life's journey over the past few days seemed distant and unreal.

Once again, he wondered why she'd keep the existence of their daughter a secret from his family while he was in Albania. Francis felt his parents' lives would have been more meaningful had they known of their granddaughter. His mother might have been harsh to Celeste, but nothing justified Celeste withholding such a huge secret from his parents.

He stood up from the bed and went to the bathroom to take a quick shower. Francis let the soap and hot water cleanse his body and help wash away the nightmares' melancholy. After showering, he put on shorts and a polo shirt before going downstairs to the kitchen.

Celeste was seated next to the kitchen window, looking outside at nature while holding a cup of steaming hot coffee. On the wooden kitchen counter, Francis saw a tray with breakfast and a cup of hot tea. He dipped his teaspoon in the honey jar and stirred it into the teacup.

Celeste looked at him, not having heard him come into the kitchen. She felt his presence only after the sound of him stirring had distracted her thoughts. She lovingly gazed at him, while he sipped his tea, hesitating to ask him anything.

"This is good. Thank you." Francis said while she looked at his profile.

"You're welcome." She replied with a soothingly soft voice.

In reality, she was scared and unsure about Francis' reaction to his nightmare. She, bewildered with what might have prompted the nightmare, had been contemplating different possible causes. Over the last twenty to twenty-five minutes, since leaving the room to allow Francis to get washed and dressed, Celeste had tried to piece together clues and make sense of the confusing situation.

She tried to think back at their words and actions during their brief reunion to better understand what the dream may have meant. Back at the coffee shop, she noticed a loss of innocence in him but knew that was perfectly normal given that he was now forty-eight and not eighteen. If life teaches all of us one thing, she thought, experiences change us all, one way or another.

For Celeste, the moments of Francis drifting off into his thoughts were reasonable, given that he was getting to know her all over again. She expected that he would think about how much of each other's lives they didn't know.

She understood that both things, Francis' loss of innocence and his desire to know her, were true and natural. However, she also knew she should not dismiss his behavior, but observe and try to understand it. Celeste played scenes in her mind, attempting to pinpoint any memories which could shed light on the meaning of his nightmare. Yet, no matter how much she thought about it, she couldn't understand the meaning of his dream.

There had been one thing. Before they left the shore, Francis rewrapped the bark with the cloth and placed it back inside the same tree's hollow from which he had found it. Celeste, still absorbed in the pleasurable feelings they had experienced, hadn't been paying attention or asking any questions. After Francis placed the engraved bark back in the tree, he turned to her with a smile and winked.

Celeste, now that they were back at the house and having witnessed Francis having a nightmare, started contemplating what might have been his motive for placing the rewrapped bark back inside the hollow of the tree.

"Can I ask you one thing?"

"Yes," he answered.

"You must think I am crazy for asking you this, but it is something that I would like to know," Celeste spoke with a steady voice. "Why did you place the bark back inside the tree?"

"Because that is where it belongs. That is where it has always belonged."

"What do you mean?" She asked with an uncertainty in her voice.

"Well, I told you the story behind it already. I carved your name when I was a child and left it there. It has been there for thirty-six years and that's where it will stay."

Her eyes bulged, and her mouth fell wide open. She did not expect such a stern answer and was uncertain how to respond to it.

"Your explanation perplexes me," she admitted.

"Perplexes you?" Francis asked, his tone low and his eyes squinting. "There was no intent to deceive if that is what you are implying."

"That's not what I am saying, Francis. There could be no deception in a child's innocent display of love on a piece of bark. There was no deception in the love we had decades ago. It would be an injustice to label the feelings we shared during these last few days as deceptive. It is your explanation that perplexes me. You act as if our whole lives and future hopes are dependent on that tree."

"Why are you making such a big deal out of it, Celeste?" His tone was more assertive now.

"I am only trying to understand whether I am still a memory to you."

"Do you think I still consider you a memory? Is that what you think?" Francis asked calmly.

"Well, am I?" She asked.

"No Celeste. You are not a memory." He sighed heavily, looking at her soberly. "It's just that sometimes I don't understand what I've been missing most in my life. There are so many different things involved and the more I try to analyze them, the more questions come to mind," Francis confessed.

"I do not know what to think! It seems as if you're on cruise control down memory lane." Celeste said with a steady and determined pitch in her voice. "As much as I would love to, I just don't understand you!"

Celeste waited for a more thorough answer, but one never came. She had anticipated that Francis would have given more direct and clear response. But instead, he responded with an obtusely abstract answer which she was unable to interpret. She felt as if her soul had suddenly become half empty. Celeste realized that the confusion and pain she was feeling reminded her of the seven years of suffering she'd endured right after returning from Albania many years ago.

"You may do it subconsciously Francis, but I want you to know what you do still hurts other people," Celeste spoke with an even pitch.

Francis looked at her and said nothing. She sensed his loneliness, hurt, or longing in his dark, mysterious eyes. Or perhaps it was a combination of all three. Celeste wasn't sure whether to hold him in order to comfort him or push him away in anger for being so emotionally distant. Should she hold him close for helping to confirm that he had passed the 'Test of Life'? Or should she push him away for entrapping their love in the distant past? "Francis, say something. Don't give me your silence because I've been tormented by your silence for thirty years. Please, Francis. Can you do that for me?" Celeste pleaded as her eyes were on the verge of tears.

"A long time ago, you told me that what you admired most about me was my mind and my appreciation for life's finer things. I appreciated life because I've had boundless opportunities to explore it. Life taught me about all types of love. It taught me to love and devote myself to music and sports equally." Francis paused, sighed deeply, and looked intensely into her eyes. "It also gave me you. Life gave me the chance to love you for you and to love all the things our love gave me. That love was relentlessly abiding, nurturing, and sustaining. Yet, it was snatched away from me along with everything else. I know that things can never be the same again, and, I blame no one else for that but fate itself."

"Fate? What do you mean 'fate?' What does fate have to do with anything that may happen from now on?" Her voice sounding more irritated now and increasingly not liking the direction his statements were heading.

Francis shook his head while briefly looking at Celeste as if he were helpless. He took short, deep breaths while staring at the floor. So many thoughts were whirling around in his mind that he could not stop himself from becoming increasingly more confused and overwhelmed. Celeste, sensing his discomfort and helplessness, tried to clarify her question.

"Fate can be beautiful and wicked over time, depending on life's shifting winds. Everyone goes through this kind of a rollercoaster, at least once in their lifetimes. But what has separated you from everyone else is that you have both a giving heart and the courage of your convictions. You stand strong and tall and confront the abyss of failure and pain."

"That's where you are mistaken." Francis picked up the teacup and felt its' comforting warmth radiate through his hands. "I used to have the heart and courage. Not anymore. All I have left now are memories. How is clinging on to those memories not a display of my appreciation for life? Do you think I could have ever survived if it were not for my memories?"

Francis paused and stared into space, then continued explaining. "In my darkest hours, I sat alone thinking life was getting a kick out of mocking me. But then, I decided to fight back. For it was at the worst possible times that I managed to live my finest hour. I always managed to pull out of the bad times because you always seemed alive and real to me, not just a faint memory." Francis again looked deeply into her eyes.

"Well, you don't have to rely on old dreams and memories to remember me anymore. I am here for you to hold, touch, and make love to." She grabbed his hands and drew them close to her chest. "I am standing in front of you. Here, I am all yours. What else do you want?"

"I can't! It has been thirty years of my life wasted and I don't know anything about you." Francis' voice cracked as he pulled his hands away from her. "I don't know anything about myself! What could have I made of myself if I had not hidden away somewhere and abandoned my life by suppressing my dreams?"

"Can you please stop talking this way?" Celeste got up from the couch and walked a few steps away before turning to face him again. "Don't you understand that nothing is ever wasted because each twist and turn in life is a learning experience that only makes us stronger? Why live the rest of your life in a distant past when you can step into the batter's box and live your life for today and every day after?"

"As much as I would love to do that, I know that I can't…"

"Yes, you can! And yes, you will!" She interjected, sitting on the edge of the desk. "I know that you have had great passions and persistence in life that few could equal. You know that too. You have a gift rarely found in others. I always remember how you never concede defeat to any problem or obstacle in your life. You are, and were, tenacious and determined. Your perseverance will get you past this point as it has so many times."

"No… It's not going to happen." His voice trembled as he looked away from her, now resigned to his conclusion about their love. "Nothing will ever be the same! I am too tired to make a difference now."

"What are you talking about? Why are you speaking like someone has just died?"

"That's perhaps because something has died inside of me since I've returned. Back in Albania, I survived with the hope that one day my goals, aspirations, and dreams would prevail. Now that I am back, it seems that the faint possibility of hope has been lost. My father and my

American way of life too." He paused for a moment as a lump rose in his throat. "And us, along with everything else."

"Us?" Celeste exclaimed.

"Yes! Us!" Francis responded. "We're not as innocent as we used to be. I always idealized our love as something pure. But the more I think about it, the more I wonder whether it might not have been real. I let you go that day on the shores of Saranda. You kept our daughter a secret from my parents. We both messed up in our own ways and now we both have to admit that perhaps our love wasn't real…"

Upon hearing these words, Celeste felt a deep pain in her soul, yet she tried to maintain a stoic facial expression. All she had wanted to do was to console him, comfort him, and help him get through these dark thoughts. Instead, she was watching him sink deeper into despair. Suddenly, Celeste felt an unstoppable urge to break down and cry, realizing that Francis considered his life a failure. A failure to execute his goals. Through no fault of his own. For Francis, his fate had not only been sealed, but fate itself was mercilessly mocking him. He sat there, staring into space pondering the implications on his future given this somber epiphany.

There was a moment of absolute silence between them. Earlier in the morning, Celeste had been beside herself with anxious excitement, believing that no dream is too small to ignore or too big to overcome. But Francis' sad reflections of his life had clouded her sunny optimism with insurmountable hopelessness and deep despair. She felt that no words could soothe her disappointed feelings. All she could do now was to gracefully drop the subject and leave Francis to his melancholy.

And that was exactly what Celeste did. She stood up from leaning on the desk, walked past Francis, and headed to the front door in the living room. But not before murmuring a few last words. "Sometimes, what one man seeks is right under his nose. But sometimes, what he wants is both difficult to grab, and painful to let go."

Francis watched her leave the room and tightly closed his eyes in incomprehensible emotional pain. Each time in the past, when he had closed his eyes, he would imagine music playing magically melodious notes, restoring in him a sense of hope and tranquility. But this time, the soothing rhythm of life, which he had always preached about to others, was deafeningly silent. It may have been shattered over the years along with many of his once indispensable values. Perhaps, twenty-nine years of continuously struggling to break free from the chains of the Albanian regime had finally gotten the best of him. Those confining chains had prevented him from fulfilling his true potential in life. Now he was forced to dwell on the disappointing reality of what he had become.

The world that Francis had known in Albania, much to his contempt, had become a dull place. A suffocating sense of hopeless fatalism had finally caught up to him. He had always been a hopeful person, but now he felt anguish for Celeste and himself. He felt hopelessly trapped with no way out. His eyes remained closed because he was afraid to face the reality that he'd been away for too long. He knew that avoiding these feelings were not going to bring back his late father or any of the broken dreams. Yet still, he resisted the impulse to open his eyes and face his life as it was.

Francis fought and fought and fought… until his determination wore him out and he finally fell asleep.

Between Two Roads

He opened his eyes. There was still some sunlight coming through the living room windows. While still lying on the sofa, Francis watched the distant horizons through the halfway open windows. He closed his eyes for a moment, wishing he could wrap his arms around all the dreams that had dominated the many sleepless nights. Sometimes his dreams had been beautiful, but now they had fallen into despair because of his disappointment and bitterness of the reality.

Somehow, Francis knew that somewhere, beyond the confining reality of his failures, there was a boundless future carrying realistic hopes and dreams. It would be an infinitely abundant future brightened by the flickering light of hope, bereft of the pessimism and self-pity currently smothering him. It was a future life, a time and space on the distant horizon, filled with joy and happiness. It was a contour of optimism that glared him now lovingly for the ages.

Francis knew that the fundamental difference between them was that while Celeste had pragmatically embraced their recent reunion, he had made small halting steps only to realize that his life hadn't been the glorious journey that he had envisioned. His confrontation with a world far removed from what he'd imagined made him yearn that much more for the life he had dreamed.

In his disappointment and despair, he had thoughtlessly spoken to Celeste, forgetting that the source of his psychological and emotional survival over the years had been standing right in front of him. All the thoughts of his life's unachieved expectations should have been irrelevant given that the world could never have been the ideal paradise he'd wanted it to be. As an idealist, Francis had always been obsessed and entrapped by his past. He'd hoped that returning home and reuniting with Celeste would enable him to go back to the happier times in his youth. But now he was beginning to realize that each experience along life's journey was uniquely rewarding in and of itself. Now he understood that his feelings of despair would only subside when he began to appreciate each unique moment life presented.

Francis got up and went to the kitchen to see if Celeste was there. He was hoping she'd forgive him for his harsh words earlier in the afternoon. Not finding her in the kitchen, he searched throughout the house, at first on the ground floor, but she was nowhere to be found. Then, with increasing panic, he searched upstairs in her bedroom. When Francis opened the door all he saw was an empty bed. His eyes wandered around for clues to where she could have gone. Then, he saw a single piece of paper on the nightstand. Francis immediately felt his stomach tighten in dreadful anticipation of the letter's contents.

Francis picked the letter from the nightstand and stared at the words while his hands trembled. He found it difficult to concentrate. He finally seized the moment and zeroed in on the words of the letter.

My Dearest Francis,

I feel like I have not known you for a lifetime. And even though I am so glad that I found you again, it still feels as if we're strangers.

A long time ago, when we were both a couple of kids in search of true love, fate, with a little bit of help, brought us together. At first, we shied away from each other, not knowing how to advance our cravings for one another. But once we kissed, once we dared to commit unconditionally, we both knew that we were meant to be.

The times that we shared were gentle and kind. We were able to allow ourselves to daydream, to wonder, and to lose ourselves in surreal romantic situations. It was during that time when our love evolved into something greater than the sum of its individual parts. Love like ours belonged in romance novels with happy endings. You brought me hope, encouragement, and joy at a pivotal time when I aspired to be a dancer against my parents' wishes. You helped me find my voice and self-confidence at a time when I still wavered in all my decisions. You made me believe that no dreams are impossible or unattainable and that no goal is small enough to be ignored. Think big and dream big, you always used to say to me.

I know that fate knocked us apart over these last thirty years and we can blame no one for that. No choices we made were wrong because no one could have foreseen their consequences. Life happened, and its responsibilities came from all different directions. You did what you had to do by helping another family and that is admirable. You risked your life to save theirs. You traded off your own dreams to make them realize their hopes of survival. And I always applaud you for that. I could never blame you for it.

But now that you're back, you still hold on to those memories as if I am not standing in front of you. Perhaps, you fault me for not telling your parents about Stephanie. I tried to explain to you my reasons. I cannot turn back the hands of time and undo what's been done.

I know you must have felt horrible and hopeless when you realized that you could not come back to New York to be with the people that you loved the most and chase the dreams that we always talked about. I know because I felt the same way when you didn't return home. Somehow, I knew that we had become mere memories of each other.

Just hours ago, when you sat there paralyzed by distant thoughts, it made me realize how you have idealized the past and are unwilling to build a future. That hurts me more than anything right now. Because I know that during the past few days, I fell in love with you again, with the man that you have become. And not just the boy you were back then.

It appears though that you are more content with the way I was then, instead of cherishing what we have now and moving on from here. I cannot make you love me if memories are the only things that are left for you. And for that reason, I cannot stay, and I hope you understand.

If in our future lives, we briefly come across each other, I want you to know that I never stopped dancing to your music. Loving you has always been the best choice of my life. Because my love for you will never die.

Love always Celeste

Upon reading the concluding paragraph, Francis looked up from the letter and stared into space. He held the paper tight while gazing in disbelief, his feelings now an extension of his emotional rollercoaster from earlier in the afternoon. When Francis first saw the letter, his stomach tightened in emotional discomfort. After having read it, he was so intensely upset that his vision became blurry.

He went downstairs and out the front door, still in painful disbelief, yet anticipating Celeste having left him. Francis walked around the house several times, like in a nightmarish merry-go-round with no end. Finally, he sat down on the porch as the full gravity of the situation sank in.

"She is gone," Francis finally whispered while looking around hopelessly. He suddenly realized that he was again on a porch sadly longing to be with Celeste. Exactly like he had been in southern Albania. He had traveled thousands of miles, just to be in the same place, recreating the prison he had struggled to escape. No longer were there political or geographical barriers confining him. Francis was now imprisoned by his own emotions and isolated by his own psychological limitations. He didn't know whether he could let go of his attachment to the past, actively embrace his present, and look forward to a happy future.

On the left, there was the beautiful lake reflecting the setting Sun and the world he had come to romanticize. On the right, there was a more difficult journey, which led to the world he had abandoned and was refusing to accept. Two opposing roads so tightly intertwined with each other and yet so far apart. Which one would he choose? Which one would help him reach his place in the Sun?

Almost three decades had passed since the last time Francis and Celeste had been together. At last, the couple was reunited after his daring escape succeeded. During their reunion, old feelings and distant memories had quickly returned like a sudden summer rain. They had changed considerably. However, the romantic memories of their youthful love were so deeply embedded in their tortured souls.

Francis had gone above and beyond his fear to escape from Albania. He always felt deprived in the oppressively crushing grip of the Albanian Communist regime, a regime that had suppressed his love for music, art, beauty, and freedom. A repressive political system that demonized and castigated his birthplace, the home to all types of dreamers. A regime that kept him from his true love. A love that could only be a gift from God. A gift manifested in the beautiful woman that was Celeste.

Now, he was more convinced that the primary reason for his escape was this true love. Along with a deep appreciation for the time they spent together. These three wonderful days with her were a rebirth of the things that made his life pure and worth living.

With eyes filled with tears, Francis stared at a faintly distant mirage of Celeste. He began contemplating what it would be like to never see her again. She had left and was never going to return. Disappearing into the dark velvety embrace of the night, Celeste was taking with her the most meaningful part of his life. His dreams.

The passage of years and his experiences in Albania had coalesced together, like two bullies, and created a schism between these two lovers that was more than physical. These two oppositional forces had ruptured their feelings, their souls, and their future aspirations together. Fond memories of their love now evoked beautiful longing and painful regret. Both in equal parts and in one recollection. When would this anguish end for them? When would life stop mocking them with its most precious gift, one's first love?

When the vision of her mirage dispersed into the dark night, he looked at the sky. There, he saw the full moon, dressed in silver clouds. Off in the distance, the crickets chirped their nightly song. Leaves rustled under the soft caress of the summer breeze. For a moment, everything seemed to be in black and white, resembling the scenes of old movies.

For Francis, the night continued to be unendingly long and hellishly lonely. This was a night of love and hope, regret, and disappointment. It was a night when his past irreversibly collided with his present and future.

2003: Back to Hopes and Miracles

The sporadic sound of firecrackers exploding could be heard in the distance. Celeste, startled by the noise, flinched from the window. In fear, she moved her hand so fast to her mouth that she knocked the journal over from her lap. She slowly picked it up, then placed it on the table. Francis' face vividly appeared in her mind as she relived old memories during this Fourth of July celebration. She felt a return to the present was long overdue. She could finally sense her heart quickening and her mind breaking free of her memories.

Celeste had been thinking about how random occurrences in their lives had stacked one against the other. She remembered their final day together at Lake George, and how it had ultimately changed them forever. How she had shut down after their conversation. She hadn't anticipated their argument, and it tore her apart. When she whispered to Francis something about 'an unknown difficult to embrace and painful to let go,' Celeste tried to compel Francis to let go of the romantic memories that haunted him. While walking out on him that day, she had a fleeting hope that he'd grab her hand and stop her from leaving. When he failed to do so, it confirmed that his life's difficulties had done irreparable damage to him. She believed the only solution was for her to separate from his life again. So, she had walked away, despite being unsure whether it was the right decision.

Celeste walked into her kitchen and refilled the teapot. She watched the muted television in the living room through the kitchen doorway. Nothing interesting had been on all day, so she was watching the Yankees silently play her Boston Red Sox. She used the silence to sift through her thoughts. Momentary recollections quickly played in her mind, but now she wondered how accurate the memories had been. The teapot began to whistle. She poured one more cup.

"How about the journal again?" Celeste thought to herself. With teacup in hand, she picked up the journal off the table and headed to the master bedroom. She sat at the edge of the bed, thumbing through the pages one at a time until stopping somewhere in the middle. Still, the photograph of the thousand words remained there. Celeste held it tight in her hands as if it were her most valuable and best-kept secret. The expression on the mysterious man's face stayed imperceptible and nearly impossible to read. And what was there for her to read when he had hidden his feelings so well for so long? How could he hide so well in a simple black and white photograph when the world boastfully operated in color?

Although many years have passed, many still wonder about the mysterious man. What happened to him? What was his final fate? In what direction did his life's journey take him? Which path did he choose? As these questions come to our mind, the mysterious man continues to conceal the answers. He does his best not to reveal himself. He revels in it. And we know by the silence that he planned it this way.

The Aging Musician

Picture a man with a wrinkled face and mysterious eyes, twenty-five or more additional years on his tab, living from day to day with little to no plans for the future. The man was the thinking type, the sort of man one would expect to find in literary books among other philosophers shaping young minds. The man was also the dreaming fellow with a knack for beautiful instrumental music that tastefully depicted human affection and infinite possibilities.

There was no question that he understood the intricate ways that music and life were connected. He listened to music to reflect on the meaning of life. He lived his life because he found musical elements in all aspects of living. He saw music in the obvious things like the piano, cello, and gramophone. But he also explored it in nature, literature, history, writing, baseball, and love. Because there was musical beauty attached to all enjoyable things in life, music transcended all facets of life. For him, music was the rhythm of life.

He made sure to keep music in his heart. The same heart where he had found his lifelong swan. The thirteenth movement became the theme of their undying love. It also became their solace in good times and bad times. He loved her without any restriction; he loved her unquestionably and deeply.

***

Francis had taken care to show his love that day, twenty-five years ago at Lake George. The day she walked away. It was nighttime. His engine roared and the streetlights were all but a blur as he fearlessly sped back to Astoria from Lake George. No obstacle was about to hold him back from again proclaiming his unconditional devotion to her. Francis had decided that even if he drove through a police speed trap, he wouldn't stop. He would drive even faster to be with Celeste, regardless of the legal consequences. He had been in such a race before while running across the border to Greece. Francis had fallen many times during that first race and injured his knee. Many times, when he could barely stand up, he had questioned whether he had the will or ability to finish his escape. Then he would be angered by his brief surrender to defeatist ideas. Back in the Albanian forest, a successful conclusion to his escape seemed unlikely. His future seemed so incredibly volatile and dangerously uncertain.

Now, the race from Lake George to Queens was much more likely to have a successful outcome. Unlike his run through the Albanian forests, this drive through serpentine highways and picturesque scenery provided Francis with a fulfilling happy goal. He knew what was expected of him and how to attain it. He could see the light of their love at the end of the tunnel. He had just been unwilling or unable to see it before now. And for this reason, Francis drove as if chased by the devil himself, while ignoring his mind's effort to trap their love in a romantic past.

The more he thought about the prospect of losing her again, the harder he pushed on the car's accelerator. His impatience was swiftly overtaking his persistence. He loved her so much that he did not mind any risks resulting from his daring action. The car swerved and swayed left to right and back again. As soon as one row of trees sped past him, he would approach another in the blink of an eye. Further down the road, nearly a mile ahead of him, there was a section of road under construction. It had been excavated and looked set to be filled in with new asphalt and gravel. Still, Francis made no attempts to slow down. He would take his chances, despite a high probability of one of his tires hitting a pothole or careening into the construction area on the side of the road ahead. If he got a flat tire, he would simply use his spare in the trunk though it could only be driven on for less than one hundred miles.

Francis knew time was of the essence. The choice to race carelessly toward her might be dangerously daunting but a necessary risk in the name of unconditional love. His decision to speed headlong down the highway was not based solely on his unconditional love for her in the past, but also on the hope for their love to flourish today and into the future. His yesterdays were long gone now, as was the image of his younger self which had to be abandoned long ago. Yet, those passions, long buried deep, had to be rediscovered and rekindled. Thus, the car could only be driven in one direction, the one that led him getting to her sooner rather than later.

Francis realized he had to let Celeste know before it was too late, that he loved her more than anything. That he wanted to be with her always. That he wanted to marry her immediately and spend the rest of his life with her. The only question that remained was whether he would get there in time to tell her all of this. The most dauntingly dire afterthought then became: Would he ever get there?

***

Having been inspired by these events, the old man found time to write the improbable story of his journey. Fittingly, he heard the silent music of his life when he wrote and discussed these life-altering moments. His will persevered; his determination lied deeper than the cascade beneath the Blue Eye. And it never mattered how deep any of his passions were buried for there was always a small flame glistening the way.

The man with the mysterious eyes believed he had been changed forever. He no longer felt pity or sorrow. He no longer dwelled on the story of the yesterdays. If anything, he used it as a reference point to move forward. The man now revealed himself with gentle and accurate precision. The truth is he had one last chapter to write. And it was this overwhelming and final display of emotions that would particularly change all our lives.

The Final Chapter

Is it possible, I wonder, for human consciousness to overcome the loss of innocence? Or for a man to completely relinquish his inescapable thoughts and finally accept his destiny.

It is winter as I ponder these questions, as I have on numerous occasions over the years. Wrapped snugly in a thick Afghan blanket and wearing a long sleeve cotton pullover shirt and sweatpants, I'm seating comfortably in my rocking chair in my old study room.

The Sun had set nearly two hours ago as I look through my large, newly painted, bay windows. The rain has not yet stopped, but it has let up quite a bit from when it had been a torrential downpour just after sunset. It was almost beautifully poetic how the setting Sun had seemed to make way for the broodingly ominous clouds to invade what soon became a placidly dull and unappealing sky. Now, the drizzling raindrops continue to make their familiar drumbeat as they fall onto the air conditioner that protrudes from the nearby master bedroom window.

The soothingly monotonous sound of the raindrops on the air conditioner's aluminum frame melodically accompanies the ticking of the large grandfather clock along the wall. Sometimes, I jokingly refer to the clock as the 'Big Ben' given the way its grotesquely large frame dominates the room. Its ticking seems to mockingly become louder as I direct my attention towards it. Then, just as swiftly, its ticking becomes muffled as my mind is diverted to the distant horizon which stretches beyond the large windows.

Here I sit, collecting my thoughts and using my imagination to capture anything beyond my large windows. The room has become colder over the past few hours, as raindrops and briskly cold air sneak through a windowpane recently cracked by the wrath of a whirling wind. I rock back and forth, trying to fight off the chills and warm myself with the motion's kinetic energy. Perhaps, also to chase my pain away.

Over the years, arthritis along with other ailments have developed in this old wretched body of mine. Although the pain had once been manageable, now I wish I have some medicine to anesthetize the physical pain made worse by the rain. Despite the agony of Mother Nature's gift to my body, I summon every ounce of my determination, stand, and walk across the hardwood floor. I pace back and forth, struggling to organize my thoughts.

I do not know where to begin. So many thoughts about life, death, purpose, the human condition, and self-discovery become tangled in my mind. As I try to untie this mental Gordian Knot, I find myself sinking into deep despair. Hopelessness often looms over those who ponder questions for which they know they will never find answers. They know it is futile, I know that too. But I'm motivated, flirting with the notion I might be the first to find answers to life's profoundly abstract and theoretical questions.

Almost all people accept life as a continuous chain of life-altering choices and self-defining events, stacked one upon another, propelling each person headlong towards either positive or negative outcomes. The optimists among us then proclaim that whatever results in these choices and events is 'meant to be', giving it a positive spin. They do not feel contempt for the hand their life has dealt them but instead seek pragmatic solutions to make the best of their current situation. Pessimists, on the other hand, re-adjudicate the event on the theoretical premise that "it could've turned out better only if...". They are stubbornly unwilling to disturb the present or the future. So, they sit and wait for fate to hand them a good outcome throughout a life that inevitably becomes stagnant and unfulfilled. In many ways, neither way of thinking is so completely wrong; people should not totally discount each one's advantages. Both worldviews have rightly realized that life is still full of mysteries which can lend themselves to various interpretations.

And then, of course, there are those that believe an afterlife follows death. Mortality is part of life, not a disruption from it. Its inevitability is unquestionable. The only question is not whether, but where, when, and how. The answer to the enigmatic question of whether there's life after death is beyond the scope of our ability to know. Thus, in great humility, I leave its exploration to religious leaders and philosophers.

The real question focuses on a man's purpose. What is the purpose of life? Do people behave in a certain way to fully achieve their unique potential or out of societal peer pressure? Does one lead a morally distinguished life out of pure altruism and a good heart or only out of fear of legal punishment? Is it possible for one to genuinely love unconditionally or is it always a transactional exercise focused on personal benefits? It is our right and responsibility to examine such profound questions. Whether or not they can ever be fully resolved, the mere attempt to find their answer becomes a journey of self-discovery in and of itself...

While I valiantly attempt to focus on these questions, I reflect on my own life's journey. How can I describe and assess my life? While it has not followed the sort of linear path I might have envisioned, I have tried to live the most appreciative and respectful life anyone could in my circumstances.

How have the events of my life affected my character? Through my life's circumstances, I have grown into a man who refused to surrender to life's obstacles. And although at several moments, these circumstances seemed to have gotten the better of me, I kept quietly pushing that extra mile, determined to persevere. Perhaps it was simply chance or time itself that tried to defeat me. But whatever the cause, it could not surmount my determination. I kept fighting as one would a schoolyard bully. Though these obstacles, which time and time again tried to deal a knockout punch to my dreams, were not of flesh and blood, I still found great enjoyment in overcoming them. Each time life would knock me down, I would pick myself up more determined, confident, and hopeful. I had in mind one driving focus, to live in appreciation for each moment of life and without fear of what my future might bring...

I suddenly stop pacing across the hardwood floor, abruptly distracted from my thoughts by Mother Nature. The percussive sounds of the rain on the roof's shingles and against the air conditioner's aluminum frame reach a heightened crescendo. Teardrops of rain glide down the windowpane in irregular, yet somehow familiar patterns...

Then as I turn to look at a journal on my bookshelf, a great feeling of sorrow slowly envelopes my mind and paralyzes my body. The happy thoughts of love and painful memories of loss combined with romantic nostalgia and past unkept promises to create an emotional torrent throughout my failing body.

As I pause and stare at the journal through squinted eyes, a vivid promise of the past comes back and teases me, in a good way of course. I pretend to fight back, convincing myself that I am too old to keep any promises. But this promise, I must fulfill as quickly as possible. Because now, I know that I am racing against time and biology in the twilight of my years. Drawn by the nostalgia, to a sentimental longing for what used to be, I find myself walking as slow as a turtle towards the desk.

There lay a notepad and pen, beautifully placed side by side. They speak to me in a language only I know, inspiring words of wisdom. Over the course of human history, the sacrifices people make for each other have always prevailed over the tyrannical oppression of freedom, any unwanted brush stroke on an acclaimed painting, any piercing thorn on a beautiful rose, and most importantly, any obstacles that stand in the way of true love. And throughout human history, people have spilled blood to have the powerful ability to convey truth by using the items lying peacefully on the table. A simple pen and paper.

While considering these things, I turn to the window again to see the picturesquely untouchable horizon, seemingly millions of miles away. I wonder if a certain extraordinary story has become as distant as those stars in the sky. The beginning and end may sound familiar, but the events and anecdotes in between make it a uniquely gut-wrenching and timeless tale.

While thinking deeply about the story and the way that it has impacted my life, I sit in the chair next to the desk and try to collect my thoughts for a few minutes. Then again, I look at the journal though it does not return my gaze. Romantically nostalgic details never cease to amaze me. With these thoughts in mind, I put on my glasses. I then pull one of the drawers and from there uncover another journal. This one is almost empty. But soon it will serve its purpose. Of this, I am sure.

With trembling hands, I open the cover and grab the pen between my thumb and index finger. While it is difficult to squeeze my fingers together, my inspiration triumphs over any unimaginable pain. Suppressing all the emotional hurt I've accumulated through my lifetime of struggles, I begin to scribble familiar words on the inside of the book cover.

Our life is not a story trying to change the world. It is not a tale of defeat or pity. It does not make excuses by re-litigating past decisions with 'could haves,' 'should haves,' and 'would haves.' This is a simple story of 'boy meets girl,' of sacrifice and unconditional love. It is simply a reflection, a mirage of a past long gone...

I look up from the pen and paper and try to make sure that my next words reflect my thoughts as accurately as possible. It is difficult to correctly convey the magical atmosphere that imbues my past in only a few pages. And though I am trying my best to write my feelings, experiences, and observations succinctly, I know that this is quite a daunting challenge.

As I mentioned earlier, I must overcome the rational constraints of both time and science. While struggling to overcome these obstacles,

I reminisce about the life-altering moments that have come to define my life's journey. Another wave of inspirational words immediately begins to come to me. I hurriedly start jotting them down.

... *If there has ever been a lesson to be learned in life, it is that we cannot choose who we love or force someone to fall in love with us.*

Love comes naturally; it comes from the heart when you least expect it. Love is not something that one sees or hears, one cannot taste it or hold it in their hands. It is not a prize, nor a toy. It is not a force to be reckoned with or taken for granted. One can only feel it in the wee hours of the morning when dawn breaks over the valley and in the dark hours when the Sun descends below the horizon. Love is the rarefied air, essential for the very survival of the human soul. Love is the precious candlelight that withstands the harsh winds of life. It soars like a shooting star, giving hope and life to shattered souls. Love comes only once in a lifetime.

If one day it leaves, please do not be sad; do not shed tears. Do not be bitter and ask whether it was worth the pain. Do not be imprisoned in emotional misery but instead embrace all the fond memories.

For that once in a lifetime of divine opportunity, love is worth all the butterflies, the waiting, the anticipation, the pain, the hurt, and the sleepless nights.

Now, having prefaced what I'm about to write more extensively, I look up a final time and grimace in pain. I have lived through many events and survived many wars, but the one constant has been my love for the person who inspired me to write this journal. This same intense and constant love will help me do the nearly impossible one more time…

***

Nearly four hours pass by as I am hurting, fidgeting, writing, and ripping up countless pages. My last scribbled words end here, so I place the pen on top of the desk, fold the papers and place them gently in the desk drawer. I remove my glasses and rub my now bleary eyes with my tumid hands. Their enormous knuckles, deep lines, and pulsating veins form a topographical map of a world long since gone. Yet, as grotesquely old as these hands might appear, they have defied the odds of medical prediction during the last several years by continuing to give me the strength to jot down short notes.

Sometimes I wonder whether it is simply luck that keeps them going or perhaps something else. But whatever it is, I refuse to allow old age to extinguish my love for the short notes. Just as I refuse to allow time to wear away my love for her.

After rubbing my eyes, I gaze at her picture. It's the photograph I look at whenever I need to be inspired. There she is, looking as beautiful as she's always looked throughout the years. Her beauty still imbues the depths of my heart.

Tick-tock, tick-tock…

I look at the grandfather clock. Its staccato ticking syncopates with the faint beating of my heart. Over the years, I moved Big Ben from the living room into the study room. Maybe because I wanted it, along with all my other sentimental attachments, to keep me company. "My friend, we have grown old together," I think to myself. "Perhaps one of us will stop ticking when it's all said and done. And most likely, it will be me."

It is almost comical how I sit here calculating my mortality. Long ago, I was told that my towering height and broad, muscular shoulders resembled Albania's northern mountains where my father's ancestors were born.

Sometimes, I wonder whether I, like my father's relatives, was groomed to be steadfastly immovable like those mountains. I have always been reluctant to take credit or brag about my accomplishments. But I cannot discount that I fought in and survived a war where the only certain thing was uncertainty. I survived an oppressive regime's interrogations and secret police and a harrowing escape with a seemingly endless journey back home. I defied everything life has thrown at me with quiet humility. I remain devoted, through good and bad times, to a vibrant determination to live life to its fullest, promote individual liberty and freedom, and stay committed and true to one's dreams.

For all these reasons and many more, I believe that I have grown into a decent human being who never takes life for granted. Some may say I'm just a wide-eyed dreamer. Others may say I'm a hopelessly naive romantic. I will smilingly admit that I'm probably a little bit of both.

Although the toned muscular body might have once resembled the mountainous terrain of northern Albania, there's no denying my current appearance is a far cry from my strength and stamina of my youth. I'm now a subdued and solitary figure, crippled by old age and nearly lifeless.

However, I cannot blame it all simply on the normal corrosive effects of time. Until a few years ago, arthritis pain from a lifetime of normal wear and tear had been easy to manage. Unfortunately, now there is a more insidious sickness growing inside of me, tearing me down. Since being diagnosed with this dreadful disease two years ago, my health has been in a downward spiral. It has stolen my vitality like a thief in the night.

During its onset, I discounted the symptoms, thinking that it was simply old age finally catching up with me. It started with my body feeling unusually weak and fatigued. Then I began to have tremors and cramping in my muscles, difficulty swallowing and started dropping baseballs while playing catch with my grandson. The tipping point came one night when I dropped the bow of my cello while playing "The Dying Swan" for my family. When it happened, it was extremely awkward and an immediate cause for alarm because I had never dropped the bow in all my years of playing. Especially while playing the one classical piece that a lifetime ago had brought Celeste and me together.

That evening, when she asked me if I was alright, I cursed in frustration underneath my breath but nodded in approval. I did not want to extinguish the happiness we were having as a family. However, later that night, I privately confessed to Celeste that it was time to pay our family doctor a visit.

After several tests, the physician diagnosed me with amyotrophic lateral sclerosis. Initially, the Parisian doctor pronounced the illness by its French label 'Maladie de Charcot.' However, as he began describing the symptoms, I realized that he diagnosed me with the same disease that had claimed my childhood hero. "The disease is caused by a degeneration of motor neurons which are nerve cells that control muscle movement. As motor neurons waste away, muscles are unable to receive messages from the central nervous system. Unable to function, muscles eventually weaken and develop twitches. Those inflicted with ALS eventually lose their ability to initiate or control voluntary movements. However, it does not directly affect a person's cognitive or sensory functions, so you will be able to see, smell, taste, hear, or recognize touch. Most certainly, it will not affect your mind. Unfortunately, there is no known cure or treatment... Ultimately, all patients succumb to the disease," I heard the doctor saying.

When the doctor dealt us the horrific prognosis, my wife and I stood there motionless, unable to utter a word. Suddenly, it felt as if my world was crumbling before my eyes. My entire being was shaken by the thunderous echo of my mortal dread. It was at that moment that I feared death for the first time.

My wife also felt as if the world was closing in on her. Celeste cried for many nights in mourning because she would lose me once again. When the doctor recommended that I enter a patient-assisted facility, as the disease inevitably progressed, she stubbornly refused. "That is my husband and my best friend that you're talking about! I will take care of him at our home."

When I heard her speak those words, I sensed sorrow and rejection in her voice. But I also heard a tenaciously determined woman, undiminished by my situation. I choked back tears as she repeatedly pleaded with the doctors that I stay at home with her. She had refused during our thirty years of separation to stop loving me. Now, she was determined to keep me close until she could dance to my music no more.

Over the last two years, my disease has advanced faster than expected. It has stolen most of my lateral movement and nearly left me paralyzed on my left side. Most days I am unable to walk across the room without a cane and my trembling hands are incapable of buttoning my shirt. My only proper meal comes from a bag, through a tube attached to an I.V. in my arm. It's quite a struggle to get in and out of bed. As my muscles shut down one at a time, I wait for this ALS thief to finally take away my ability to breathe. The ultimate effects of this eventual outcome need no explanation.

Despite my physical regression and inevitable fate, my mental acuity is better than ever before. My dire outcome does not faze me anymore. I'm now more concerned for Celeste than for myself, so I try to spend time with her whenever possible. Though she has always been a strong-minded woman, she still sometimes breaks down in tears in moments of weakness. It must be excruciatingly painful for her to know that there is no possible reprieve for my death sentence and that she will one day lose me to this dreaded disease.

Remembering my experience in southern Albania, when I thought that I had lost her forever, I try to offer words of encouragement. I tell my wife that losing someone sometimes requires a willingness to continue searching for them in places beyond rational understanding. Losing a loved one sometimes requires summoning enough strength to tunnel through mountains to carve a path towards hope. Most importantly, it demands that their affection fully possess their heart and soul. The kind of unconditional affection that people display when the love of their lives might be slipping from their arms and leaving them in loneliness. "I only say these things because I believe," I smile at her. "Though this disease is terminal, I'm not afraid anymore. I'm not afraid to die because I know death can't stop me from loving you."

Friends and family say that I have been dealt a terribly unfair hand by life, but I disagree. Over the last 60 years, the greatest role on the world stage has belonged to two 16-year-olds in love. I have realized that no distance, no matter how many continents separate us, could keep our souls apart. Our love could overcome any obstacles. As a dying man, I consider myself, like Gehrig so aptly said on that sunny 4th of July in the Bronx, the luckiest man on the face of the Earth.

Who wouldn't consider it a privilege to have been fortunate enough to watch the most beautiful woman on the planet dance to Camille Saint-Saens' music or have been witness to his love defy life's trials? Who wouldn't be honored to have had the love and respect of friends and family or have seen his daughter grow into a strong, beautiful woman and his grandson play baseball with such passion? Most importantly, who wouldn't feel divinely privileged to have found a once in a lifetime love twice?

I'm just a simple man remembering times long past. As I face the twilight of my life, my hands are painfully stiff and swollen and my body is cold and achy when the weather changes. I have held on to her with every breath and heartbeat and that has been the most rewarding aspect of my life.

On that hot and humid summer's day, 60 years ago, I fell in love with Celeste and since then my love for her has continued to march through time. The fire of passion in my heart has never quelled and can never be extinguished. Though my patience and wisdom have grown with age, my love for her then, now, and forever remains unchanged. For love, like energy, can never be contained or destroyed. Even today I tell her, "I will always move mountains to be with you, my love, because I love you more than anything".

On most evenings, I look out the window at the park across the street where loving couples walk hand in hand. Now that the rain has gone, young and old gather, as they do every night. In the winter, they are wrapped in heavy coats and long scarves. It reminds me of many years ago when my wife and I would walk beneath the moonlit sky.

Our outings at night were always more appealing because that was our chance to escape from our daily lives and lose ourselves in green open spaces. We found simple details in nature that nothing else could overcome. The sound of crickets chirping, the wind whispering through the leaves, and the ocean splashing all allowed us to forget the noise and commotion of life in the city.

Unfortunately, now our walks are rare because I seldom can leave the house. This damnable disease has confined me within these walls and chained me to a cane and a rocking chair.

Despite all of this, I don't regret that I'm stuck at home with a failing body. Although I do sometimes crave escaping into the wonders of nature again, I've channeled my remaining time and energy to a promise. A haunting promise from the past...

Many people make promises, and, like many rules, they are often bent and sometimes broken. But not this promise. It's too special to me to be cast aside or forgotten. I'm determined to keep my promise, despite old age and the dire reality of my medical prognosis. It is a promise so innocent, and yet so consuming.

When I told my doctor, several weeks ago of my promise, he said it would be impossible for me to keep. He believed the physical constraints of my disease would prevent it. It is understandable he would say this since the disease has degenerated almost every muscle in my body. My left leg and right arm are completely immobile, and my hands are both nearly paralyzed, rendering me unable to hold a pen and incapable of playing a tune. It would go against his professional training to believe that someone in my condition could overcome medical reality.

Doctors specializing in ALS all agree that a patient's ability to move ceases when the central nervous system no longer sends electrical signals to the muscles. They all say ALS is irreversibly degenerative and inevitably leads to paralysis. Once a limb is unable to move it is impossible to regain movement again.

Despite all these medical realities, nothing is impossible. Beyond human understanding, there are infinite possibilities and miracles for those who refuse to give up hope.

I have written this evening in my study, as I do every day. I do so neither to revive my nearly paralyzed hand nor to keep my mind sharp. I write this evening solely to uphold my promise to her.

But why is this promise so important? What could possibly trigger me to reject the medical reality of my health so vehemently? Why muster enough inner strength to prove to myself and others that miracles of love can conquer scientific certainty? What exactly is this promise?

My promise started accidentally five years ago while visiting an old friend in Albania…

After the fall of the Berlin Wall and the end of the Cold War, many people in Eastern Europe called for the abolishment of their Communist-controlled governments. The events in Germany gave hope to a new generation of intellectuals, eager to move their countries in a new direction. Albanian intellectuals began putting the pieces in place to bring about the collapse of the Albanian Communist system.

Unlike the forty-seven years of the totalitarian regime in Albania, this new dawn of freedom in the region began to allow tourists to freely travel in and out of Albania.

Five winters ago, Celeste and I decided to take advantage of the opportunity and visit the southern shores of Saranda, hoping that I'd reunite with friends I'd left behind me in 1969.

Among other people, I met Nikolla, my best friend through my worst times. We hugged each other like lost brothers, just as we had done on that night in Konispol, just before my escape.

Among other things, I learned that he was dying of heart-related complications. After several unsuccessful surgeries, Albanian doctors had told him that his chances of survival were slim to none. They recommended that his only chance of survival would have to come from a surgical operation in some of the finest cardiac hospitals in Western Europe, where medical technology was far more advanced. According to them, even in the West, the surgery would likely be unsuccessful. Nikolla opted to stay in Albania and thus forgo the surgical procedure altogether.

If something had gone wrong during the surgery, Nikolla would have passed away regretting not doing so in Albania. He wanted to die in the country that had given him a second chance in life.

During his last days, Nikolla showed me his hardcover journal, worn and faded with time. In the journal, along with neat handwriting on pages yellowed with age, there were numerous letters, each addressed with a different date.

"What is this?" I asked him.

"I want you to read it. It is something that I started to write after you escaped. I missed our discussions on various topics, so I turned to writing. Eventually, it became convenient… and safe."

Nikolla had written a journal. His writing style was eloquent and unique. The language was clear and concise. I imagined the old man seated at his desk day and night. The writing contained information about his life well before he met me. Nikolla gave vivid depictions of his childhood. The circumstances around the murder of his entire family in Kosovo. His arrival in Albania where he created a new family on its southern shores. His admiration for what he believed was an unpretentious egalitarian government. And finally, being disillusioned when finding out it was otherwise.

"This is my final word," he said to me. "The word of a dying man."

Not long after, he passed away.

The thought of Nikolla extensively describing his past intrigued me, puzzled me. It captivated me because he never struck me as the type to write a journal. Although I knew he turned to writing in his journal in the absence of a close confidante with whom he could speak, I had a feeling that there might be another reason.

I asked my wife, after Nikolla passed away, the obvious question. "Why do some people drastically change their behavior after living their entire lives in a certain way?" She smiled at me and gave me a simple answer. "Because it is never too late."

"Too late for what darling?" I asked her.

"Secrets soon become muted. And as time passes, they become buried somewhere in our hearts," she told me.

Although I expected a more verbose reply, I knew she was absolutely right. Celeste has always believed everyone possesses the skills to overcome life's barriers. Her answer helped me understand the timelessness of the written word. It can commemorate special moments and enable people an outlet to express gratitude for the gift of life. At that moment, I silently promised myself that, before I left this world, I will write my final say as well.

Here I sit, five years later and that promise still stands. I have religiously written in my journal, trying to reconstruct my past. Those life-altering moments that would otherwise become vague recollections if it weren't for my promise to her. I am writing perhaps for the last time, proving once again that miracles can happen. I have found strength in these hands once again.

Fortunately, the nature of this disease is such that it does not impair my mind or memory, so I have been able to think long and hard about what I want to write in this final chapter.

I have found, more than ever, great comfort in my writing. In understanding the tremendous solace that comes from chronicling a life filled with unconditional love and an endless devotion. This is what I hope to convey to Celeste in writing my final letter, finished just moments ago.

I'm trying not to dwell on the finality of it right now. For I see my piano, which has grown old with me, along with my grandfather clock. I slowly stand up from the desk, assisted by my cane in my left hand. One of my feet feels so heavy while standing, I jokingly wonder whether there is a bucket of cement hanging from it.

When I finally reach the piano, I sit and slowly play old familiar tunes. My fingers can't strike the keys as crisply as they once could, so some musical notes sound broken apart while others are muddled together. But I tenaciously play on, unfazed because nowadays it's my desire for soothing beauty of music and not quality that comforts me. It is my passionate love for music that keeps me playing. After all, I have always been a determined musician.

I have been a lover of all types of music for as long as I can remember. Over the years, I have come to realize that the beauty found in music transcends all facets of life. I have discovered that beauty in the obvious things like the piano, cello, and record player. But I have also found it in nature, literature, history, writing, baseball, and in the greatest of all, love. Because you see, there is musical beauty attached to all of life's most enjoyable things. Music is the rhythm of life.

While thinking of this, I turn to look at an old friend. Perhaps, the friend for whom I have the most sentimental attachment. It sits there in a corner, having not been abandoned after all. It appears to glow gloriously mocking all the years that condemned it in silence. I deeply crave, now more than ever, to glide the bow over its strings. Oh, how I want to give that old devil one more try. But my fingers have locked again. Today, my dutiful writing has worn me out and there is no more gas in my tank.

***

It's been nearly three months since I last played the cello. That day, as I began playing the first somber notes, she walked in just as gracious as ever. Her hair soft and long, her timeless face looked at me with loving awe. While she stood there, admiring my perseverance to play despite the pain, I could almost hear her thinking, "You'll always be my Saint Francis."

She silently watched me play without even pausing to acknowledge her presence in the room. Then, amidst small hand twitches perceptible only to me, I suddenly lost my grip on the bow and watched it fall to the floor. This had been happening intermittently over the last two years. Celeste walked over to me, picked up the bow and placed it between my fingers. Then she lovingly helped me guide the bow over the strings. She kissed my forehead and gave me a tight, warm hug. "I love you, sweetheart," she said, though I could hear the sorrow in her voice.

Remembering playing the cello for the last time that night always brings tears to my eyes. But I can't dwell on that right now. Realizing that I have almost no energy left, I slowly shuffle to the desk, take the folded letter out from the drawer, and slip it inside an envelope.

Then, I see a small yellow stack of post-it notes on the desk. Instantly, an idea comes to mind. "Old habits die hard," I smile to myself while peeling a single post-it note from the stack and stick it on the envelope. I quickly scribble on it, "Just so you won't forget me tomorrow!" My mission could never be complete without the finishing touch of a note with an old saying. I grin and groan.

I get up from the chair, shaped over time by my heavy frame. I start limping slightly as I feel a great heaviness dragging my left leg. But I refuse to allow any of these damnable symptoms to stop me now. I am Don Quixote, the fictional knight from literature, who in the name of his imaginary lover, dedicated his life to literature, chivalry, and most importantly love. Armed with a cane and an envelope, I march forward to my lady, awaiting me in the bedroom which we have shared now for many years. Infused with an endless love, burning passion, and eternal dedication, I sally forth through the house to give my beauty the letter, my declaration of love for her.

This envelope, this post-it note, the journal, and all the notes over the years sum up all our romantic starry nights. They depict the labyrinthine nature of my life, a life filled with hopes and desires. They constitute my understanding of love and provide insight into my often mysteriously complex character. Through my writing, I have battled against impossibility just to remind her that absolutely nothing can or will stop my love.

After reaching the master bedroom, I open the door and shuffle in. There she lies in the bed that has been ours for so many years. Since it appears she has fallen asleep, I walk slowly in order not to wake her. I want to slide the envelope under her pillow, but it is nearly impossible not to make noise because of these cursed uncontrollable feet. The floor creaks loudly underneath every step. I frustratedly assume it is only a matter of time before she hears the noise.

My assumption turns out to be accurate because I notice shifting movement underneath the blanket. She rolls over and looks at me with a mixture of affection, concern, and surprise. She has caught me red-handed like an officer nabbing a burglar. Standing exposed in front of her with guilt, I try to quickly hide the envelope beneath my sweater. A sudden smile expands across her face as she calls out, "Francis, you're back."

She gets out of the covers wearing a light red sweater tied around her delicate shoulders. She eases my pain with her eyes as she runs her fingers through her long beautiful grey hair.

"How are you feeling, sweetheart?" she asks me.

"I am alright. Could be better. But could be worse," I answer.

"What were you doing until now?" She smilingly asks me.

I can recognize that sly smile from a mile away and now realize I can't hide for much longer. Revealing to her the envelope, I look at her helplessly, wanting to be wanted, wanting to be loved and adored by the one who carries the secret key to my heart.

"I should have known it. All those days you acted so emotionally distant, I had a feeling that something was going on," Celeste confesses, anxiously anticipating the contents of the envelope.

The first thing that she notices is the yellow post-it note. She reads the old inscription and drifts off for a moment. I can almost feel her heavy breathing. "Oh darling," she exclaims, her voice trembling with excitement.

She then opens the envelope and removes the letter inside. After unfolding it, Celeste pauses and begins reading the words, which have come to epitomize my recent defiance against life's improbability.

Fifteen minutes go by when she's finally finished reading the letter and looks up to me. Her eyes are filled with tears as she gets up from the bed, walks toward me and hugs me.

Moments later, she kisses my lips lightly and asks if I want to dance. For reasons I do not understand still to this day, I blush every time she asks me to dance. Then, as she hums Billie Holiday, she extends her arm forward to invite me to get up from the chair. I feel her touch like I never have before, and now yearn to be held that way until my last dying breath.

We embrace close and dance slowly, as Lady Day sings to all the hopeless romantics, grieving through "I'm a Fool to Want You." My wife's tears wet my cheeks and I can almost hear her sob as she sways slowly to my rhythmic movements. She has been a tower of strength all these years, but now I wonder if she has any energy left to fight for me, 'til the end. And yet, as we hold our faces next to each other, she does not forget to run her hands occasionally lovingly through my now white hair.

"I am so sorry darling," I whisper to her.

"Sorry? Why are you sorry?" she whispers back.

"For not having been able to bring more happiness to your life."

Celeste pauses for a moment, stares at me deeply with those wet hazel eyes, caresses my aged cheeks, and gives me an answer that makes me feel light on my feet.

"Once, long time ago, you told me that a man's dream is to defy time. He will use anything unimaginable, even if it means that he must claw his way to that finish line. Only a miracle would allow him to reach that point in life. Our love created a miracle of that sort. That miracle was burned brightly every moment since we first met. Our story is a miracle, for it is timeless. You've always been my happiness and I wouldn't trade any of our moments with anything else in this world." Her sobs become louder now almost as if she were angry that I would say such a ridiculous thing. "What an old fool I am," I think to myself.

I hold her head with my left hand and lay it on my shoulder, as we continue to dance to the song. Then, I say the only thing that feels right, the only thing that has felt right through all our years together.

"You were right many years ago. We have met before in previous lifetimes, and we will always keep coming back together."

Now, she leans a little backward and looks at me, waiting for my next philosophical remark. Instead, I say the one sentence that comes from my heart, the only thing that is profoundly true. "I know for a fact that it happened three or four times only during this century."

She looks down, blushing, as we embrace each other tighter and dance once more until the song ends.

We sit in our bed.

"There is certain magic that transcends everything else," she says.

"There's something unusual about love that can heal the soul of an ailing man," I counteract. "Love and magic are inseparable sides of the same coin. Yet only dreamers dare believe in the magic of love."

Celeste sighs and looks at me with a blank expression.

"Do you really think that?" Her lower lip starting to shake as she bites down on it.

I nod.

Celeste takes a deep breath as she sniffles hard and tries to regain a measure of control.

"Long ago, you told me a tale, a legend about an Albanian warrior, who whispers only when he dies. A warrior with a wound in his heart. He awaits the fate of his impending death to come. Yet, he refuses to give in. For there is one last thing he must do. You said he fights his last battle with death for that one final moment. The mountains pause to listen, and the world mourns. Driven by his love for another, he saves his last breath. He saves his last breath, just so he can whisper to her his song one last time."

Instantly, I fall back when I hear her. "What do you think that last whisper would be?"

"I believe that it is a reminder."

"A reminder? A reminder of what?" I ask.

"A reminder of all sorts of things. A reminder of love. A reminder of sacrifice. A reminder of where, when, and how. A reminder that it is never too late!" She speaks.

With a puzzled face, I walk slowly to the bed and place the now empty envelope on top of the nightstand. I lay there beside her and then we lovingly hold each other as we usually do every night. Then our tongues slip to heavenly places and dance about effortlessly. Irregular movements at first until our tongues finally begin to rhythmically move together.

And that is how it always starts.

The Last Whisper

My Dearest Celeste

Many lifetimes ago, there was a beautiful young girl, who looked me straight in the eyes and told me that she'd dance to my music forevermore. She placed her hand on my heart and never let it go. Later, she told me she loved me and asked me to make a wish. The wish I made was that both of us would never, ever leave. I never consciously knew then, but at that moment I somehow instinctively understood, that love, like many of life's other mysteries, could never be conquered. The love I hold for that girl will never, ever die because she'll always be my one true shiny dancing star.

I write this letter by candlelight at the piano in the old study room where we first made love. And though that first act of love is in our distant past, I can still feel your soft body pressed against mine, your hands wandering in search of unfamiliar places. And even today, I know that it was that touch then that sparked so many wonderful memories for us. During the years without you, that same touch helped carry my heart above my lonely existence to divinely heavenly places. For I know that it was the warmth of your soul itself that has always given me the breath of my long life.

From here, I can see my old beloved gramophone, which has followed me through my life's journey, sitting languidly on top of the desk. It has been my trusted friend even through the times when I had to keep it hidden underneath the wooden floorboards of my house in Albania. I would only free it from its cold earthen prison each time I needed to see your smiling face in my mind's eye. I can still picture Fred Astaire singing and gracefully tap dancing on the silver screen as he surrendered himself unconditionally to his endless love for Ginger Rogers.

Oh Heaven, I'm in Heaven,

And my heart beats so that I can hardly speak,
And I seem to find the happiness I seek,
When we're out together dancing cheek to cheek.

Or I can still hear Lady Day singing one of our favorite tunes to comfort all the world's hopeless romantics. Oh, how I can still feel that majestically melodic voice resonating down to the very depths of my heart, as I think about you, my dearest Celeste.

I'll be seeing you,
In all the old familiar places,
That this heart of mine embraces
All day through.
In that small café...

Do you remember how our small café brought us together over the years? And how we held each other as we danced to our song?

Now that I sit here and wait in the sunset of my years, I am reminded of the many things you have given me in life, especially your love, your passions, and an extraordinary child.

Why do I love you so much? Your love has touched me in ways that no one could have imagined possible. Your words have struck me with emotions I have never experienced. When I asked you during that Fourth of July years ago if you could dance to my music, I meant it then as I do now. When you placed your hand on my chest, I saw in your very eyes, that you'd love me always. And it was that love which I have carried with me until now and will forever.

And how can I describe what your passions have meant to my life? They have been the source of my strength for as long as I can remember. The bicycle rides, the walks, the movies, the baseball games, your love for ballet, the old café, the kisses, the lovemaking are things that I cherished always. And I want to thank you from the bottom of my heart for all your passions that carried me through life, just as I want to thank you for your faithful determination to restore Café Place. I have been amazed at your sentimental attachment to our little coffee shop and even more so with how you have expressed those feelings in your essay to me so beautifully, and yet so succinctly.

And what can I say about you as a mother? As I try to find the words to describe how great of a parent you have become, an ancient Albanian myth comes to mind and reminds me of how you have sacrificed nobly as a parent throughout your life.

**

A long time ago, there was a young lady in Northern Albania, who was asked by her village to sacrifice herself by being immured. They believed her lifetime confinement would appease the gods and stop the carved stones in the village castle's walls from crumbling. She touched the hearts of many locals when she sealed her fate by telling them that she'd agree to be immured only if they met her conditions. She demanded that they leave one of her hands exposed so she could caress her newborn baby, one of her breasts accessible to feed her infant, one of her legs so she could rock his cradle, and one of her eyes so she could witness her child grow up.

You were a struggling single mother when you raised our beautiful child and provided her with all the important things in life. Just like that young mother in the Albanian tale, who selflessly thought only of her newborn, you were a tower of strength for our daughter all while your own hurt feelings were not being nurtured. In the most critical years of your life, you gave her the warmth of a splendid mother, the memories of a lost father, and the education that molded her into a fine mature woman. And what a great job you have done. Look at her now. She is a successful lawyer and strong woman.

When I look at her now, I see you. She has your character, your mindset, your energy, your devotion, and your passions. And look what a beautiful family she's built and what a fine boy she's raised.

One day I asked her to sit beside me. I wanted her to know how you and I got together and how we had been separated many years ago. I told her everything filtered through the prism of my heart. She cried and threw her arms around me and said, "Oh daddy, I know you. I know you more than you think I do. I always knew you because mom always talked about you." That made me smile as bright as the Sun. It made me smile because, during all those years, you had not forgotten about me, just as I had not forgotten about you.

The most regretful thing that I did in my lifetime was to agonize over long memories when the primary person for which I had been longing was staring me right in the face. There was no way I could ever let you go a second time. I would have never forgiven myself for that because I know that what we have is extraordinary. Love like ours has been built on the unpretentious ground since its beginning. Our love is pure, unconquerable and brave.

When I found your letter that last day at Lake George, my whole world shut down because I suddenly realized that I was about to lose you this time for selfish reasons. Potentially losing someone I dearly love because of controllable factors would be too bitter a pill for me to swallow. And for this reason, along with my deep and abiding love for you, I did what I had to do and came to the coffee shop, hoping that our favorite café would create yet another miracle. And indeed, it did.

Now I sit here and await the inevitable, yet still, I remain optimistic. My enduring love for you still gives me hope to go on and explore in places where the human imagination cannot reach. My endless love for you feeds me the strength to move mountains, in hopes of holding you, my sweetheart, in a place where we both will have eternal happiness. My love for you roars from the depths of my heart and strikes a lightning bolt of emotions through every part of my old aching body in ways no one could have thought possible.

We had a wonderful life together and how I wish it never had to end. But soon I will be gone, that I know, for this dreadful disease does not discriminate amongst those inflicted with it. But no matter where or when it claims me, please know that it will never take away my love for you, for death could never tear us apart, my dearest Celeste.

With all of this in mind, I have only one thing to ask you. When my body finally gives way and I become unable to move or speak, place my cello next to our bed. And I promise you, that even when I am finally gone, I will still carry the torch of our love and play the cello for you. Will you please dance to my music then?

Because of my eternal love and affection for you, I wrote you this letter, not simply as a declaration of our love, but as a reminder that your presence in my life has always been a miracle in and of itself. The kind of miracle that most people seek their whole life and never find. Consider this letter a beginning with no ending to this life's love we have chosen. Or simply, a beginning with no end. This is my declaration of love for you! This is my last whisper!

With All My Love,
Francis

Epilogue

He fell unconscious the following week and three weeks later he was laid to rest. But not before Celeste had fulfilled his last dying wish and placed the cello next to him in bed. She saw that he must not have suffered long given that his face had such a profound expression of tranquility. Perhaps, his soul floated away with the music of the swan in his heart.

Over the course of the next four years, Celeste visited his grave regularly and brought a fresh bouquet of tulips because they were always his favorite flowers. She then ever so gently caressed the photograph of him which was attached to the gravestone as her eyes welled up with tears. She remembered many summers ago when she had first fallen madly and passionately in love. Their story showed what started as the flickering flame of a teenage summer romance eventually burned brightly through all their years and withstood all ferocious winds of their life's trials. And eventually, that tiny flame grew into a roaring inferno of love that time itself could not conquer.

Then, one night, she lay in bed, unaware whether this was the night for a miracle. She had visited his grave earlier that day and placed fresh tulips there as usual. But suddenly, while caressing his photograph, she heard the faint sound of a cello playing. Celeste thought as she looked around, it must have been her imagination, but the musical notes sounded so real. Upon her return home, Celeste went up to the attic and searched through all the old photos, letters, and anything else she could think of from the past. She wasn't sure what she was searching for exactly, but she had a strong urge to look. Celeste had just about given up looking, convinced that she was being a silly old woman. Then, she'd reached behind a stack of photo albums and pulled out an old dusty envelope with a small yellow post-it sticker that read "Just so you won't forget me tomorrow." Celeste, kneeling there amidst the years of photos and mementos, cried her eyes out while slowly reading Francis' 'Last Whisper.' Celeste, hours ago, went to her desk and wrote a letter of her own. Now she's lying peacefully in her bed with her letter folded neatly between her hands and her chest.

My Dearest Francis

Today I asked God if it is possible to find you one day. He told me to be patient because everything in God's plan comes at its proper time and in its proper place. With tears in my eyes, I begged God to take me to the time and place where I will be at your side again. So that I could be with you, and you could hold me tightly in your arms. Just as you used to in our favorite café, in our bedroom beneath the sheets, or under our favorite ancient oak tree. Yet again, God told me to remain strongly focused on tomorrow and each day thereafter rather than those precious bygone memories. I impatiently asked if he would ever help me. No more excuses, God! After all, is he not the omnipotent & almighty God, who tells us to care for one another, to forgive one another, to help one another, and most importantly, to love one another?

Again, God gave me an unsatisfactory answer. "Wait!" He spoke. And I have waited. All I do is wait! I wait and wait and wait. No positive encouragement or poignant words of wisdom will ever bring the desired closure for my heart and soul. I am a bystander of my own life, just watching time pass while anxiously awaiting my turn to escape my world and come to love you in yours.

My sweetheart. My love for you will remain endless. You were a great man, a genuine man with a heart of pure gold, unafraid to challenge people, and relentless in your love and passion for life.

Francis. I know that during your thirty years in southern Albania, you never stopped thinking of me. If I could go back in time, I would erase all the sadness you felt borne from the dark melancholy of those many lonely years. Please always be mindful, that though we were physically apart, I never abandoned you because you never escaped my heart and mind. I held you and cherished the memory of you in all my thoughts every day.

When you came back home, and we saw each other after all these years of separation, I found a reason to live again. But then there came a moment of weakness when I faltered under pressure, particularly when you were drawn to your distant thoughts. I faltered then because there were moments when looking at you reminded me of my own distant thoughts, filled with painful longing and sorrow. The love I have for you always haunted me and I guess at the time I did not know how to effectively deal with that. I am so sorry I hurt you when I walked out at Lake George. I'm ashamed of myself for doing that because I had no right to take away your fond nostalgia for the past. You've never imposed any conditions on me, and it was wrong of me to impose any premises on you. I realized my mistake as soon as I came home. Then I cried my eyes out because I knew that no matter how hard I tried to fight it, nothing in this world could erase my love for you.

When you came looking for me at the café and asked me for my forgiveness, it killed me on the inside knowing that you blamed yourself for something that wasn't your fault. I tried to convince you that you were not at fault, that it was instead the result of my irrational decision. Regardless, you went on feeling culpable and while your eyes were drowning in tears said: "I can never imagine another lifetime of you not dancing to my music." I instantly threw my arms around you and wanted to hold you endlessly. Through your sincere words, I realized at that moment what I had known all along, that love pure like ours awakens the heart and enriches the soul.

You have taught me that the best kind of love is the one that starts from the heart, grows within the heart, and ends with the heart.

That is what you have given me in all our years together. That is what I hoped to give to you in return. Now I am a swan searching for you, wanting to take another glimpse at you, the love of my life.

Recently, my sleepless nights have increased in number and reminded me of all my lonely nights in Astoria. Back then the question of 'what is love' used to haunt me night after night. It was a question that I asked myself every morning upon waking up and every night before falling asleep.

The first word that would always come to my mind in the morning was your name, Francis. I found myself asking the same question over and over. Why was your name the first word that came to mind? After a while, the answer became painfully apparent. Your name was the last word I thought of before going to sleep. But then why would your name be the final word on my mind before going to sleep? Was it because I loved you so much that I could not imagine a minute passing without thinking of you? I loved you endlessly, as I do now, and will until the end of time. But why? Why do I love you until the end of time? What does it mean to love and be loved? What is love? Is it developed through a long-term process? Or is it possible that love could blossom overnight like a desert flower after sudden rain?

In my case, my love for you started that very summer I laid my eyes on you. You were the perfection of God to me. He must have poured the whole of his purest talents in you to make such inner and outer beauty. During that summer beneath the trees, when I stared at your innocent smiling face, all I wanted to do was kiss you forever. When I held your hand, all I wanted was hold it forever. When I looked deeply into your dazzling brown eyes, I saw and felt your heart and soul and all I wanted was get lost in them forever.

That was the answer. The answer to all my questions. You were my love at first sight. It was a love that came from a lonely heart, a heart that had been locked away for too long, a broken heart that had been crying in secret for too long. When you came into my life, you made me believe again. You made me believe that I could do anything. During days together in late summer, beneath the endless blue skies, you liberated me once again. You came to my rescue and allowed me to open the gates to my heart and let you in unconditionally. And how could I not? You were and are everything I have ever wanted. You had the piercingly dreamy eyes that saw right through my heart. You had the soft hands that touched my soul, you had a face that could make me melt away; you had the warm smile that made me love you forever.

As I contemplate my feelings for you, night falls as the Sun descents beneath the distant horizons. I sit by the window and count the stars, including Lady Day. Their number does not equal more than the amount of my love for you. And then I close my eyes for the night. The last word that comes to mind is your name, Francis. Wait for me. I shall see you soon.

I love you,
Celeste

Instinctively, Celeste touched the heart-shaped locket attached to her old necklace. She unsealed the envelope and took out the final piece to Francis' last whisper. She held in her hands the dried bark from the ancient oak tree which had her name carved on it. This last piece of the puzzle which had innocently started everything for him. She now remembered their first bicycle rides. She envisioned how, sixty summers ago, a young Francis had marveled at the way she danced to the music of 'The Swan.' She vividly pictured their first kiss in the rain after her ballet performance. How they danced to the song "Cheek to Cheek" during one of their stays at Café Place in September 1939. In her keen memory, she remembered their visit to the Blue Eye and Francis' dark brown eyes as he wished they could be together forever and ever. She recalled their reunion, their weekend at Lake George, their wedding night, and their trips around the world.

Now the miracle was beginning to finally take shape. The miracle which she had believed in her heart but dared never speak out loud. The last whisper brought it all together for her. In her weeping eyes, she saw Francis, young and timid, playing the somber melody of the swan.

And now, in the end, the swan was fluttering the wings for the last time. She closed her eyes gracefully, her face with an expression of calmness and tears no more, as though she knew that Saint Francis had arrived at last.

Which was exactly what was happening. Her Francis was playing the cello for his beloved swan one last time.